southside sinners

BOOK 2 OF THE CULTURES COLLIDE SERIES

KEITH ROMMEL

MILFORD HOUSE

an imprint of Sunbury Press, Inc.
Mechanicsburg, PA USA

MILFORD HOUSE

an imprint of Sunbury Press, Inc.
Mechanicsburg, PA USA

For information about special discounts for bulk purchases, please contact Sunbury Press Orders Dept. at (855) 338-8359 or orders@sunburypress.com.

To request one of our authors for speaking engagements or book signings, please contact Sunbury Press Publicity Dept. at publicity@sunburypress.com.

FIRST MILFORD HOUSE PRESS EDITION: September 2025

Set in Adobe Garamond Pro | Interior design by Crystal Devine | Cover design by Amber Rendon| Edited by Jennifer Cappello.

Publisher's Cataloging-in-Publication Data
Names: Rommel, Keith, author.
Title: Southside sinners / Keith Rommel.
Description: First trade paperback edition. | Mechanicsburg, PA : Milford House Press, 2025.
Summary: The two girls, a CPS worker and a police officer, work hard at trying to right the wrongs of the world they were subjected to. But, twenty years later, the two girls are catapulted into a second war with the Southside Sinners.
Identifiers: ISBN 979-8-88819-407-2 (softcover).
Subjects: FICTION / Horror | FICTION / Thrillers / Crime.

Designed in the USA
0 1 1 2 3 5 8 13 21 34 55

For the Love of Books!

For Bryan McGonigal

We have unfinished conversations left.
We have stories to tell, laughs to share.
Your struggles are heard,
and your fight is strong.
Remember, you are stronger than it.

contents

CHAPTER 1

what happened

"I'M INTERESTED IN knowing how it all came to an end," Emily said. Her young, smooth skin shone in the sunrays that beamed in through the open window. Her lips sealed shut as she looked at her mother, who had aged dramatically in the past few years—a fact both difficult and painful to acknowledge. To see a parent, the epitome of strength and courage, become weakened by the unseen, slow, ticking hand of time chipping away at her life-source was hard—even on the bravest of people.

Emily stuck her thumbs underneath the bulletproof vest she wore and shifted it. She hated it, but Captain Creighton required that all officers wear one. The reason didn't need to be explained.

"Mom, I know you've kept this hidden deep down inside for a long time, and I've respected your need to keep the details of the event from Hannah and me by not looking at the case files, but I think it's time I hear what happened. I need to know."

Stefanie's wrinkled face was overtaken by sadness. Her eyes welled with tears at the firm stance and request from her daughter. Her hands wrestled with each other. Memories that were probably better left crushed and tossed away, never to be spoken about again, came bubbling to the surface. She sat at the kitchen table accompanied by a heavy sigh, and Emily sat next to her, eyes fixated, concerned, locked on her mother.

"I'm sorry," Emily said. "I've upset you and shouldn't have asked you. Especially like that."

"No, it's OK," Stefanie said, and her expression softened, cracked a smile even. "You have a right to know, and it's about time I break my silence about it. I didn't ask you to stay away from those files and not tell you or your sister for any other reason than I wanted to protect you. Protect you from the horrible things that had happened. But you're grown now. Both of you. So fast. And you are right. You need to know, and I have no right to keep it from you."

Emily reached across the table and held her mother's age-spotted hands. "I know you protected us and raised us well. I thank you for giving me and Hannah the best childhood two kids could ever hope for. We didn't feel like the kids with the dead parents they showed on every news channel in America. We only knew your love and clung to that. It was all we needed."

Stefanie smiled, and Emily massaged the backs of her mother's hands with her thumbs, trying to comfort her.

"I remember that day as if it were yesterday," Stefanie said, her voice cracked with emotion.

Emily continued to rub her mother's hands, waiting to hear the story. She lost her breath as she felt the pound of her heart quicken at the thought that she was going to relive that final moment with her mother.

"After the man named Beto killed Officer Buckley and his wife, he simply walked away. He had no idea they had taken me in and that I was in the house. I happened to be in the bathroom, and Buckley had given me a gun for protection. I expressed my fear of the gang and the possibility of them getting me. He told me to carry the gun with me, and I did. When I heard the shots and ran out of the bathroom, I couldn't believe what I saw. Buckley and his wife were dead. Shot down in cold blood. He was near the doorway, flat on his back, and she was slouched on the couch. There was so much blood." Her hands trembled, and tears streamed down her face, but she made no crying sounds.

Emily clamped down on her hands, trying to lend her strength.

"I ran out of the door with the gun and caught up to the killer from behind. I hated him. Hated what he had done and what I had seen and been through. The loss of your uncle, mother, and father . . . it was all too much. I hated so much that I was no longer myself. The hate I felt had changed me. I had become the monster every member of that gang was. I pointed the gun at the back of his head, my aim dead center. I couldn't stop my hands from shaking, but yet I looked forward to pulling the trigger."

"You don't have to continue," Emily said. "You can stop. I don't like seeing you like this."

"I need to continue. This is for me now," Stefanie said, and she blinked hard; the tears rolled down her cheeks, wetting her wrinkled face. "I wanted to shoot him so badly, and all I could think about was revenge." She fell silent. "All the spilled blood, loss of life, and for what? A chance encounter. A mistake? Maybe fate had a sick sense of humor." Her red eyes focused on Emily's. "I miss them all. What happened was senseless and could have been easily avoided." Stefanie wiped her tears. "This cry feels good. I haven't allowed myself to do this in a long time."

"I'm sorry I made you cry."

"You didn't do anything," Stefanie said and rubbed Emily's hands too. "After I pointed the gun at his head, I squeezed the trigger. When I heard the empty click, I squeezed the trigger over and over. Beto turned around and laughed at me and just stared with this stupid grin. I'll never forget his face. The crooked smile with the yellowed teeth. The blank, soulless stare. I was in shock that the gun had no bullets and didn't know what to do. I mean how was I supposed to kill him?"

"Do you know why the gun didn't have bullets?"

"I've wrestled with that question every day for so many years. I think Buckley gave it to me as a sense of security. Maybe he was afraid that I was going to try and hurt myself . . . I don't know."

Emily thought. "After everything you'd been through I can understand why he did that. I might've done the same thing."

Stefanie smiled, but the story that needed to be told chased it away. "Beto merely pushed the gun aside. He told me that the next time I was to point a gun at someone, I should make sure it's loaded. He simply walked away with a laugh, and I never saw him or heard from him again."

"Wow," Emily said. The surprise forced her to stand. A swell of emotion came over her. But, as always, she managed to hide it, keep it inside. She shifted her vest again, distracting from her discomfort. It was her job not to show weakness for the sake of her aunt and her sister, Hannah. She needed to be the pillar. That was her job, and she had been doing it ever since the moment she saw her father in that wheelchair, paralyzed, alive with the beat of his heart and yet dead to the world. Her thoughts trailed. "I wasn't expecting that."

3

"Me neither," Stefanie said. "I thought he was going to kill me, and in that moment, I really didn't care. I had lost everything except you and your sister. I knew I needed to survive for you two, so I could take care of you, but I know I wasn't thinking clearly. A mind wrapped in anger and having a thirst for revenge makes you careless. I believed I had lost everything there was left to lose, and I fell into myself, defeated."

Emily sat and tried to swallow the lump in her throat.

"But I was wrong. I had you, Emily. I had you and Hannah. You two are what kept me going all these years."

Emily licked her lips, her mouth dry. "I know you did everything within your power to protect Hannah and me. It's really strange that I never wanted to ask you about what happened between you and this Beto because I knew there was too much pain there. I didn't want to do this to you."

"They did this to me, not you."

Emily could see a smile trying to force its way out.

"You've known though, haven't you?" Stefanie said.

Emily hesitated. "Known?"

She nodded. "Why I had to keep it a secret?"

"Of course I knew," Emily said and held her aunt's gaze. She and Hannah had been calling their aunt Stefanie 'Mom' for as long as Emily could remember. "But I've been looking at your sadness since I was a kid." Emily scooted forward on the seat. "I know I don't tell you this much, but you did a great job raising us. Especially knowing what happened and what you were left with. I understand you had to bottle everything up—even yourself—to try and protect us. But you can let that out now. Let it go. You've swallowed the poison and held it in for far too long."

"You do the same," Stefanie said and settled into a heavy cry.

Emily let her mother mourn. She had earned that right years ago, and now Emily would stay with her until she calmed.

"I have to tell you something," Emily said softly. "This might be difficult for you to take in."

"What is it?" Stefanie said and choked back her tears.

"We have reason to believe that the Southside Sinners are on the rise again."

"What? How is that possible?"

"The gang symbols are starting to appear again, and there's been a spike in robberies, break-ins, and civilian assaults. The Sinners are making no attempt to hide the fact that it is them."

Stefanie centered on calm. She looked at Emily, seeming to appraise the uniform she wore. She brushed her fingers across the badge. "You wear this so bravely, like your uncle did. He would be proud of you. So would your parents."

"I know they would," Emily said and adjusted the utility belt around her waist. Her gun hung as heavily on her hip as the despair had on her heart. But the badge on her breast pocket shone just like her strong sense of responsibility, a beacon of hope for those in need. It was a responsibility she didn't take lightly. "If these thugs think they're going to rise again, they're mistaken. Severely. We're going to beat them down before they can get any footing."

Stefanie's expression became stern, her voice that of a guiding parent. "If this is some of the original members, you need to be careful when you deal with these people. They are cold and have no regard for anyone or anything. Nothing is off limits to them, and the more desperate they are, the more violent they will become. These are things I could never convey to you in my stories because it is one thing to hear about it but something else entirely to experience it."

"I'll be careful," Emily said and squeezed her mother's hands to reassure her. Stefanie squeezed back.

"I'm proud you decided to wear the uniform to stand up against the thing that has troubled you the most. I won't say how concerned I am about your safety because you'd just shoo me away. But if anything were to happen to you or your sister, it would kill me."

"Nothing is going to happen to me or Hannah. I promise you that. We feel the same way about you. We want you around for a long time to come."

Stefanie chuckled. "I don't know how long you expect me to stick around. I'm getting older by the minute, and my body aches something awful."

"Are you taking your medicine?"

Stefanie nodded.

"Have you?"

"Yes."

"Have you seen the doctor?"

"Yesterday."

"That's right. How did that go?"

Stefanie shrugged. "OK, I guess. There's been no change."

A flicker of dishonesty appeared in her mother's eyes. Emily wouldn't dare call her a liar though. She always tried to protect them even if that meant dancing around the truth. "That's good. Maybe it has stopped spreading?"

"I think so. I start another round of treatments in a week."

"Hannah and I will be here with you every step of the way."

"I know you will. In the meantime, you have work to do. Keep people safe. Get those thugs off the streets and into a cell."

Emily nodded. "OK," she said, patting her mother's hands as she stood. "I'll stop by tomorrow and see how you're doing. I've got to get back out there."

"Be careful, and don't forget my warning."

"Always, and I won't," Emily said and walked out the door with her mother's sadness emblazoned in her mind; the burden of knowing the truth had settled into her shoulders and neck.

The Southside Sinners had taken so much from her childhood, from her life, and her family. In those who survived, the Sinners had left a gaping void that could never be filled. She could see that in herself and her sister—had seen it throughout the years.

That was the devastation the war had left behind. A war that had been waged in the streets of the town that had earned the nickname "Battleground." Given by the media all those years ago, to this day, it still remained and, it seemed, for good reason.

CHAPTER 2

mother and son

HANNAH CLIPPED HER ID tag to her breast pocket, grabbed a manila folder from the passenger seat, and exited her vehicle with a hard sigh. She hated what she was about to do because she knew no matter how well-intentioned this decision and process might have been, she would be looked at as the bad person.

In her short career, she had heard it all: Homewrecker. Bitch. Devil. How could you? Do you have a kid? Do you know what it's like? Have you no heart? I'll get you for this!

Yes, the things people said hurt her and bothered her well after her shift had ended, but she would never show it and would never let her fiancé know either. It was her choice to do this, and the broken hearts left in her wake were just a part of the process. Oftentimes she needed to remind herself of this.

She believed she was a good person and made a significant difference in people's lives. That people needed her help. Maybe they couldn't see it in that moment because it was all so very traumatic, but if they would take a moment and look at the bigger picture, allow the wound to scab over and heal some, they would see it was for the best.

When she reflected, that's when all this madness made sense. She got up every morning and went to work for the greater good, tried to wear a smile of a righteous warrior, and never to think anything negative about what she did. It was the only way to keep going. To wear a suit of armor to deflect the negativity.

The whole reason she entered into family affairs was to help the helpless. To give a voice to those who couldn't speak for themselves. She wanted to protect the innocent, as so many had tried to do for her and her sister, Emily, when the world was on fire around them.

"Are you ready?" Officer Henry Frerk said as he climbed out of his patrol car. His sun-leathered face with white rings around his eyes from constantly wearing his sunglasses made him look like a raccoon, or perhaps, a reverse image of one. He put on his glasses and immediately looked the part of an officer fully in charge of his post.

"I'm as ready as I'm ever going to be," Hannah said, feeling safe next to the six-foot-plus man. She looked at Officer Frerk with a smile. The uniformed police officer had a pug nose, gray goatee, and a receding hairline. Nothing had changed about his appearance since the last time he'd escorted her to serve someone their papers. So why did she look at him like it was the first time every time?

It was something else to focus on, besides her nerves, she supposed. A way to try to ignore the heavy pounding of her heart and the tremble in her hands.

"Don't give me that," he said and clapped her shoulder. "I know this is hard, but we didn't create this situation. They did."

"I know," Hannah said and looked at the house as they approached. The single-story home was in shambles. Shades in the windows had broken slats and hung tilted in their frames. The paint on the house flaked, the lawn was bare, and the driveway was cracked and treacherous. "Look at this place."

"It's a shithole," Officer Frerk said in a whisper. Algae covered one side of the house that was heavily shaded and didn't see the sun. "I think the green shit on the side of the house is helping to hold the walls together."

"Like glue?"

"Yeah, now you're getting it," Frerk said.

Hannah laughed but quickly covered it up. Her professionalism was so very important to her.

"I know this one's not your case," Frerk said. "I was out here two weeks ago with Jamie."

"Yeah, Jamie." She sighed and shook her head.

"Why are you here?"

"I was told to be here by my boss." She paused. "That's the only reason I'd be here."

"Sick call?"

"More like 'I'm sick of dealing with the shit' call."

"Well, they send the good ones out for the tough ones."

"Is that what it is?"

"That would be my guess."

"I have a boatload of my own work to do. When Paige told me I was coming here to serve the papers . . ." Hannah huffed.

"That's what bosses do. They delegate. Why do you seem so nervous?"

"I'm always nervous. You're the only one with the ability to pick up on it. I don't know, I guess I'm unsure how this is going to play out."

"Well, reel that nervousness in. I'm here to help you and protect you. But if you weren't chosen for being good at what you do, I wonder what you did to piss your boss off."

"I don't know, but whatever it is that I did, I should apologize."

He laughed. "Yeah, maybe you should. This woman is a bit mouthy and can be a real bitch, so just be ready."

"I've heard it all before," Hannah said. "But I'm glad you're here with me. You make me feel safe."

"If I let anything happen to you, your sister would kill me."

"Big growl with hardly a bite."

"Being you said that, I know you haven't seen her in action like I have."

They stopped in front of the rickety door, and Officer Frerk knocked.

"When you said you've heard it all?" Frerk said and rocked on his heels. "The first thing I thought was, 'not like this you haven't.' Trust me." He folded his arms and chuckled. "You'll see."

The interior door swung open, and a heavy woman with no bra and a worn, partially see-through t-shirt, long stringy hair, and no makeup answered the door. "What now?"

Her nipples showed through the flimsy material. They were big and dark.

"Vicki Daraio, we would like to speak with you and Urban, please," Hannah said in a gentle tone.

"I'm not letting you talk to my son," Vicki said. "He's a minor, and he doesn't like the police, and he certainly doesn't like whatever the hell you are, lady."

"My name is Hannah, and I work for CPA."

"I'm changing your first name to 'Go Away' and your last name to 'I Don't Give a Shit Where You Work.' So why don't you go and do just that? And while you're at it—" Vicki lifted a breast—"you can suck on this."

"Please, Vicki, don't make this harder than it already is," Frerk said and stepped between the women. "Last time I was here I told you I was going to lock you up for disorderly, and even though you pushed and pushed I gave you a break. I'm reminding you of that because I want you to remember how nice I am. But today . . . today we're going to do things by the book. Now call your son out here or I'm coming in."

"You ain't coming in my house!"

Hannah reached around Frerk and held the manila folder out for her to take. "Court order. We can come in, and you cannot stop us. But I'm asking you nicely. So please, let us in, and let's get this over with."

The screen door creaked as it opened enough so Vicki could reach her thick arm out and snatch the folder away. She looked through the pages.

"This is bullshit! Who wrote this crap?"

"Your case manager."

"Well, where is the bitch? Is she afraid to face me?"

"She's out of the office today. She's sick."

"Sick from what? A guilty conscience from trying to steal people's children away from their parents?"

"You have a legitimate court order signed by a judge. Now please, get your son."

"Urban," Vicki shouted. "Come here!"

Frerk stepped aside, and Hannah watched Vicki take out her cell phone to make a call.

"Yeah, I have CPA at my door," she said into the phone. "It looks like they're here to take Urban away from me."

Urban came to the door and stood next to his mother. He was just as tall but toothpick skinny.

"Yeah, well the police are here with her. The same guy as last time," Vicki said into the phone.

When Urban saw the police officer and Hannah, his shoulders went limp and he sighed. "Not these people again."

Vicki put a hand on the mouthpiece of the phone and said to her son, "Damn hunters. They're gonna take you away."

"Huh?"

"They're like damn predators," she said, resuming her phone conversation and ignoring Urban's confusion. "You stumble, and they pile on you until you can't stand anymore. And once you're down, they tear into your flesh and don't care that you're screaming out in pain." She listened. "I can't not just let them!" She listened some more. "Yes, I understand." She hung up the phone.

"Urban, can I get you to come outside please?" Hannah said, but his mother threw out her arm to block him from stepping forward.

"Vicki, you need to stop," Frerk said. "You're not making this any easier, and you're not going to do your son any favors by getting locked up."

"So I'm committing some sort of crime because I'm trying to let him know what you two are gonna do to him? There's something wrong with you people." She lifted her other breast. "This one is for you."

Urban looked at his mother, and she crossed her arms and looked away. The boy opened the door but remained inside the house and refused to look at Hannah or Officer Frerk.

"Urban, you are going to be coming with me and this nice police officer. I'm going to be placing you in temporary custody of the state."

"There is no such a thing as a nice police officer," Urban muttered. "And I don't know who you are, but I know you're here for no good reason."

Frerk closed the gap between himself and the teenager.

Urban's eyes, two dots of disdain, focused on Frerk and then slowly moved to Hannah. "I'm not leaving my home or my mother. You can't make me."

"I actually can," Hannah said, conjuring a soft voice. "I'm going to have Officer Frerk escort you to your room so you can grab a change of clothes and a few items you may need. Please cooperate. This is hard enough on you and your mother."

"And like you give a shit!" Vicki said and stepped outside. "Is someone trying to take your kid away? And don't stand there and tell my kid how I feel. You have no idea how hard this is on me. None!"

Hannah refused to engage with her.

"Do you want to take him to get some items?" Hannah said to Frerk.

Frerk escorted Urban into the house. Hannah followed closely behind. Down the cluttered hallway and into a small, messy bedroom they went. The house smelt of marijuana and appeared as though it hadn't been cleaned in years, making the outside seem more hospitable and livable than the inside. Now Hannah knew for certain her being here was necessary. This boy needed someone to speak up for him.

She could feel Vicki's burning stare on her back, and it made the tiny hairs on her neck stand on end. "Mrs. Daraio, can you please back away? I don't want you standing so close to me. You're making me feel very uncomfortable."

"Yeah, sure, whatever," Vicki said. "Even my body heat offends you. You're one of those people that is sensitive over everything, aren't you? I can tell you that you're nothing special to be around."

Hannah watched as the boy gathered some things, crying as he did so.

"Look at what you're doing to my son. You don't know who you're messing with," Vicki said under her breath.

"Excuse me?" Hannah said. She turned square, standing up to the much larger woman. "Are you threatening a county employee?"

"I don't know who you think you are, thinking you can come into my house and take my child away. What do you want from me? Do you expect me to stand here and feel nothing? That's my son!"

"Ma'am, I didn't work your case, and I know who he is. I'm here on behalf of my colleague and the order of the court. You're going to have to contact your caseworker, and she will give you any information you might need to get this problem resolved."

"You think this is a problem?" Vicki said. "A problem!" She laughed. "I can't believe that's what you called it. You're the one splitting a family apart. I'd say you're the one with the problem."

"I want to make something perfectly clear. I didn't do anything," Hannah said. "Not to you or your son."

"Oh, you did and are," Vicki said and smacked her hand against the wall.

"I can't have you carrying on in front of your son like this. The situation is tense enough, don't you think?"

"I don't know," Vicki said. "It seems you don't think I have the capacity to think for myself or my kid."

"Just stop. Seriously. Your carrying on doesn't change what is happening."

"I'm not carrying on," Vicki said. "You haven't seen me start to carry on. Brought your bodyguard. Made sure you did that, didn't you?"

"What's your problem?"

"You. And if you keep that smug tone with me—"

"Enough!" Frerk said.

"Yes, enough," Hannah said. "I need you to control yourself in front of your son. You need to set the example starting now so this is only temporary instead of permanent."

"So now you're going to teach me how to parent my kid?"

"No, I'm asking you to watch your behavior in front of him," Hannah said. "He's clearly upset, and so are you."

"No shit, genius! I have every right to be upset!"

"Why don't you go over to him and comfort him and tell him everything is going to be all right instead of focusing all of your anger on me?"

"OK," Frerk said and held Urban by his arm. "He's ready to go."

"Are you going to let me talk to my son before you take him away?"

"Yes, but let's get him outside first and into the back of the car," Frerk said. "We're not doing this in here. Especially because of the way you've been acting."

"This isn't an act, and you're carting him off like he's some sort of criminal."

"No, we're looking out for his safety and well-being. There's a big difference. Look at this place! Send the right message!" Frerk said as he led the boy outside.

"What about my place? You knock on my door and tell me you're taking my kid away! Just like that? A damn abduction. How is that even possible? Now you're putting him in the back of a police car, and he's obviously scared and confused, and you're looking at me as if I'm doing something wrong because I'm pissed off that you're taking him!"

"I didn't create this situation, and neither did your son," Hannah said. "Again, I ask you to handle this as maturely as possible and reassure your son you will see him again soon. All of the contact information you need is in the papers I provided to you."

"I hate this lady," Vicki said to Officer Frerk. "Tell her to shut her mouth and stop talking to me. I hate her face. Her stupid little suit and skinny legs. The makeup and the perfume she wears. It's all as annoying as shit."

"Let's not start turning it into this again, Vicki," Frerk said and helped the child into the back of the patrol car.

Vicki's phone buzzed, and she looked at it before returning it to her pocket. She looked at Hannah, and her eyes drifted to the identification tag clipped to the caseworker's shirt. "Hannah Bebout," she said. "I'll remember that for sure."

"Vicki!" Frerk shouted. He grabbed her wrist and twisted it behind her back, pinning her against the patrol car.

"Get your hands off of my mom!"

"It's OK, Urban. It's nothing," she said.

"I hear something like that come out of your mouth one more time and you're done. Do you hear me?"

"I'm not sure why you're being so sensitive. I didn't threaten her," Vicki said and relaxed. "I just told her I'm going to remember her. There ain't nothing wrong with that. Maybe inspiration for Halloween or something. You know, I can dress up like a witch or something."

"I'm closing the door," Frerk said and let Vicki go. "Now get yourself together. Get over there and hug your son before it's too late."

Vicki hugged Urban, whispered something in his ear, and then kissed him. She stood upright and looked at Hannah with a harsh stare that almost made the social worker cower.

"I hope you're happy. You must like breaking up families, Hannah Bebout," she said and backed away. "Your case or not, you got the kid, so you must be happy. I hope you sleep well at night doing these sorts of things to people," Vicki said as she walked backward toward her house, never taking her eyes off the caseworker.

"Wow," Hannah said and shook her head. She turned and walked to her car. "You were right, Frerk. Now I've heard it all. I'll follow you," she said and opened her car door.

Vicki gave Hannah the finger as she pulled away. "That's for you, homewrecker!"

CHAPTER 3

visual verification

BETO HOPPED OVER a fence and ran through a back yard with some of the Sinners in tow. Chino, Manny, and Ernesto kept quiet and followed Beto's lead. Beto's heart pounded, and his hands shook at the news he had received from Vicki. He dove underneath an evergreen tree, and although he kept plenty of distance between himself and what was happening at Vicki's house, he had a clear view of the police officer and the woman from CPA.

Through his binoculars he focused in on them, committing their faces to memory. He looked at his boy in the back seat of the patrol car and clenched his teeth, grinding them with anger. He saw Vicki reach into the car and hug their son.

"Here," he said and handed the binoculars to Ernesto. "There's a cop and someone from CPA. I want you guys to see what they look like and remember their faces. They think they can just swoop in and snatch someone's kid? No." Beto shook his head. "There's a price for that. Hurry it up. I don't think we have much time to work here."

Ernesto handed the binoculars to Chino.

Beto took his cell phone out of his pocket and sent a text to Vicki:

get her last name

"Ernesto and Chino, I want you guys to follow them and wait for my call," Beto said.

Chino handed the binoculars to Manny. "Here, amigo."

"Chino," Beto said. "You're on Urban. I want to know where they're taking him."

"And what about the woman?"

"Ernesto, you follow that *perra*. If she stays with the cop, that's great. If not, stay back. No matter what, don't let her see you following her. I told Vicki to get her last name. We can find her easy enough." Beto turned away, taking the binoculars from Manny. "I think they might've awoken the sleeping giant, guys. I haven't felt like this in a long time. This shit right here, what they're doing, it isn't right." He pounded his chest. "They're hitting me here and it hurts. For every action there is a reaction."

"There is and will be," Ernesto said.

"Get ready for war. I feel it coming again. We've laid low long enough, staying quiet for the most part. No more. I think it's time to remind these bastards who the Southside Sinners are. It seems they have forgotten."

Ernesto and Chino hurried away, and Manny slapped Beto on the back and said, "I've been waiting for this."

Beto looked at Manny with a hard stare. "Good, get all the guys together. We meet in an hour, we plan, we attack, and we get my son back. We do this fast and hard. We send a message to everyone involved in this."

Manny nodded. "*Ojo por ojo*."

"Eye for an eye is right. Then they owe me a bit more for traumatizing my son. I'll take that back in my pound of flesh. It's time Battleground lived up to its name again."

CHAPTER 4

the past and present collide

BETO HAD WAITED for the cop car and the small vehicle the woman was driving to depart before he came out of hiding. He entered the worn-down house in a hurry and found Vicki sitting at the table sobbing into her hands. He placed his arm around her, and she was stiff to the touch.

"Everything is going to be all right," Beto said.

"How can you say that?" Vicki said, not looking up, her body rigid with anger, hatred, and frustration. "They took our son from us, and I had to stand there like a useless piece of shit while they did it. The poor kid was terrified, and there wasn't a damn thing I could do. Some mother I turned out to be."

"Hey! Don't you talk like that, you hear me, mamá? He's going to be fine, and you'll get your chance at that bitch. I'll deliver her to you. Would you like that?"

Vicki looked at Beto. Her eyes were sad but fueled by a deep rage that was yearning to be released. "More than you know." She wrung her hands. "Did you get here in time to get a look at them?"

"Yeah," Beto said. "I know exactly what they look like, and so do the guys. They're out doing their thing right now."

"Good. Make them pay. Make them feel the way I do right now."

"Oh, I will—you can count on it. I have Chino following the cop and Ernesto following the lady from CPA. Manny is outside keeping watch."

Vicki slammed her fist down on the tabletop. Clutter fell to the floor, blending in with the other junk strewn about the room. "I wanted to punch that smug bitch right in her face. Who does she think she is, coming here and taking Urban from us?"

"She's a damn homewrecker dressed in a nice suit, that's who she is."

"How do you just take someone's kid and live with yourself? The entire time she's telling me how to parent my child," Vicki growled. "If that cop wasn't standing right next to her, I swear I would've smashed her face in." She wiped her eyes. "'Go over and reassure your son everything is going to be OK,' she said to me . . ." Vicki's eyes flashed. "How can I do that when I know the system is so screwed up that someone like me doesn't stand a chance? What is this, some third-world country or something where they can knock on your door, force you to open it, come inside, and take your children from you?"

"They think they have the power, but they're going to find out that they've made a terrible mistake by coming here," Beto said. "Ojo por ojo. Did you get her last name like I asked?"

Vicki nodded. "Yeah, I got it, and I'll never forget it. Corrupt bitch hiding behind an escort, wielding paperwork drawn up by a broken legal system. Her soft voice and plastic face and stupid name—Hannah Bebout. Ooh, it enrages me!"

Beto felt his legs weaken, and he used the table to keep himself from falling. "What did you just say?"

Vicki looked at Beto, confused by his sudden shock. "I said she hides behind a cop and the system is broken. What's wrong with you?"

"No, what did you say her name was?"

"I said her name is Hannah Bebout. Why, what's the problem?"

Beto collapsed into the nearest chair and ran his hand through his long, graying hair. "I can't believe this shit." He sat back hard. "What are the chances?" He rested his elbows on his knees and heaved a sigh. "Get me a beer, would ya?"

Vicki got up and went to the fridge. She retrieved the beer and set it down in front of Beto. "What the hell is wrong with you? Why are you acting like you've seen a ghost?"

"Because you may very well have."

"What is that supposed to mean? Are you tweaking or something?"

"No."

"Well, you're acting weird," Vicki said and sat down and wiped her tears. "What you said, about me seeing a ghost, what's that supposed to mean?"

"The woman that took our kid just so happens to have the same last name as the doctor and police officer the Sinners went to war with all those years ago. They were responsible for almost eliminating the South-side Sinners altogether."

Vicki shook her head. "That's impossible. It had to be a coincidence. She was young. I'd say she was in her mid-twenties—younger maybe. Pretty, but I wouldn't tell her that. I can undo pretty with these." Vicki held up her fists. They were wide and meaty. Nothing feminine about them at all.

Beto gulped the entire beer. "The last name 'Bebout' isn't common, and this is no coincidence. She's at just the right age for it to be one of the doctor's twin daughters. What are the chances that a woman with the same last name just so happens to show up at our doorstep to come and take our boy out of the house? And she has the same last name as the family we were at war with?"

"I don't know."

"I do. *Cero*," Beto said and crushed the can. "I think they came and took Urban as retaliation for what happened so long ago, and they might've found me."

"You're serious?"

"Do I look like I'm kidding?" Beto shifted in his seat. His eyes wandered as he pounded one fist into the palm of his other hand.

"That doesn't make sense," Vicki said. "Wait, why would they be looking for you after all these years? You'd virtually fallen off the face of the earth. Laid low for so long and only recently came back into town."

Beto shrugged. "I've been careful, but recently I've had some of the guys doing break-ins and small robberies, tagging our territory again and replenishing some of our capital."

"Why would you do that?"

"Because I'm a leader of a fucking gang, Vicki, not a coward!" Beto said. "We're not making enough money selling the drugs. We need to expand. Leave our footprint to scare others away. We're not small time like these other guys, and I felt it was time to start sending that message. I need to close their shops and take what is ours. You think I need approval from you or something?"

"No, of course not. But shit, Beto, you don't need to get nasty with me. I've just been through some shit myself. I was the one here when they took him out of the house. I had to watch that. That traumatized me."

"Get me another beer."

Vicki stared at Beto, her eyes furious over his dismissal of her feelings. "What the hell do I look like?"

"My damn woman—now get me a damn beer!" He palmed his face. "I'm not going to tell you again."

Vicki got up and did as Beto said.

"As strange as this sounds, I've been expecting this and have even been preparing for it."

"For what?"

"The police. I knew I'd have to face off with them pricks again sooner or later. The life I live just makes that so. But they wanted to take my kid and go dirty. There are lessons to be taught here."

"Well don't just sit there and talk about it." Vicki's face was red and contorted with ire. "Do something about it, Beto. Our boy is out there in the hands of some strangers, and he's scared half to death. You need to find him, and you shouldn't wait to send a message either!"

"Shut up, would ya?" Beto said. "I said I had a plan, but I still gotta think this through." He drank some more. "I need to be careful but forceful. Send a message that we're here, and we'll paint the streets red if we have to."

"Don't talk to me like I'm some piece of shit on the streets, Beto. I just lost my son."

Beto smacked her, and she shrank back.

"He's *our* son! You should watch yourself and know who you're talking to."

Vicki's skin flared red from his handprint.

"You don't know when to shut up, and you push me to do things like that. Do you think I want to hit you?"

Vicki shook her head.

"You need to learn when to shut the hell up. Now keep quiet. I have to make a phone call," Beto said. He took his cell phone out of his pocket and called Chino. "Hey, what's he doing?"

"He's still in the station," Chino said. "I'm waiting on him."

"Good, they're probably pushing some pencils, and that'll buy us a little time. Call me when you have an update."

"I will."

Beto hung up and called Ernesto.

"Where are you at?"

"I'm outside that lady's apartment."

"Good. Is she alone?"

"No, there's some guy there with her. He's probably a husband or a boyfriend or something. Scrawny little shit."

"He might come in handy. Remember exactly where she lives. I don't want any mistakes. When we hit, it's going to be hard and fast."

"Don't worry. I've got this."

"I know you do. You're one of my most trusted. You can come back now. Knowing where she lives is good enough for me for now. I'm at Vicki's. We're going to have a meeting with all of the guys. The meeting needs to happen immediately. Give everyone a call, and let them know it starts in forty-five minutes."

"OK."

"Did you see anything else?"

"No. I don't know where they took your boy though. He wasn't with her after she left the precinct."

"I just spoke to Chino, and I'm guessing Urban is still at the precinct. Chino's tagging that cop. He hasn't left yet so we'll find out where they're moving him. In the meantime, we've got to prepare something to let this lady know she's crossed the wrong path and that the Sinners aren't to be toyed with." Beto laughed and stood. "Oh my, I have the perfect thing in mind to get this started. This is going to hurt."

"Good, Beto. They need that. I'll put the call out, and I'll be there in a bit."

"Hey, Ernesto?"

"Yeah?"

"Make sure you obey the traffic laws. I don't want any unnecessary attention on us until we've retaliated. And I think we're going to need all hands on deck for what is to come."

"Understood."

CHAPTER 5

grave site

EMILY AND HANNAH stood at their parents' grave site. The silence that had encased them for the past five minutes was filled with sadness for a childhood that had been fragmented by senseless violence. The question of why had never been answered, and each twin carried it with her—even into adulthood.

Why did they have to see the things they saw? Why had they been deprived of their parents' love? Why were people so violent by nature? Why did it feel as though the graves beneath their feet held a portion of their love hostage?

The badge Emily wore was proof that people needed protection from other people. Did evil exist in the world simply because immorality had become rampant? Why did people cast love aside so easily and give a push or a shove when oftentimes a hug would be perfect?

"I can't believe it's been almost twenty years," Hannah said. "I still feel like that broken little girl looking at Dad in that wheelchair."

Emily rested her hand on the butt of her gun. "I don't even want to think about that." She looked into the breeze. "Even though I don't remember them much, I don't want to focus on that. They deserve better. I wish they were here so they could see how we turned out."

"They don't have to be here to know that," Hannah said.

"Yeah, well, I'd like them to be here."

"Yeah," Hannah said. "Me too."

Emily knelt and picked overgrown grass and brushed away dead leaves. "I'm sorry, I didn't mean that to come out so mean and selfish.

I know you do too. I know how much their passing has affected you throughout the years. But when you look at what we could have been and what we are?" Emily looked at Hannah and smiled. "I'd say we did OK."

Hannah knelt next to her sister and helped tidy the grave site. Her fingers fell into the beveled letters of her mother's name, and soon, into the dates of her birth and passing.

"Mom, I want you to know that Aunt Stefanie has done a great job of taking care of us. I hope you don't mind we call her 'Mom,' too. She made sure we did well in school and kept us out of trouble. She made sure we focused in college and that we hung out with the right people. She worked really hard to shield us from the violence you had to endure."

"I know she misses both of you terribly, and Uncle Glenn too," Emily said. "I went to see her yesterday, and she mentioned you all. That's the first time she talked about you in a long time. I could see the sadness in her eyes. As much as she's tried to hide it, she's hurting really bad."

"You know she's not doing well?" Hannah said.

"Yeah, that too," Emily said, turning to her sister and then back toward the graves. "She has cancer but never lets on that she's in pain or that it bothers her. I think she's scared. She won't talk about it though. I hope you three can look after her. If there's a way, maybe you can ease her worries somehow?"

Hannah crawled to the next grave site and began to clean the debris away from their uncle Glenn's resting place.

"I think the Southside Sinners are regrouping and becoming active again," Emily said. "Crime is on the rise, and the gang symbol is popping up all over the place. That stupid devil's tail at the end of their SS tag . . . it makes me furious. Reminds me of things I'd much rather forget."

Hannah turned her attention to her sister. "Mad or not, you need to be extra careful out there."

Emily stood. "I don't suppose it's any different than any other day on the job. The gang symbols, the violence people act out on one another— maybe I'm looking too much into it. It's probably just some thugs trying to resurrect some old gang that died away a long time ago, leaving a big stain on this town and a void in the hearts of two little girls. A gang that you—Mom, Dad, and Uncle Glenn—were responsible for dismantling."

Hannah looked at her twin sister, shielding the setting sun with her hand. "You probably shouldn't tell Aunt Stefanie about that. You know how she worries with you being a police officer."

"Your job is way more dangerous than mine, sis. At least I have this," Emily patted her gun. "You walk into the lion's den armed with a clipboard and pen."

Hannah shrugged. "Not a big deal when I have one of your kind with me while I'm delivering the news."

"One of my kind, huh?" Emily smiled. "That almost sounds biased. Should my feelings be hurt now like everyone else's?"

"Political correctness." Hannah laughed and stood. She hugged her sister tightly. "Yeah, I think that was a shot to your character and your kind."

"And what kind is that?"

"Blue."

"Blue, huh?" Emily punched Hannah playfully on the arm. "Shut up. You're as gentle as they come. That's why you do what you do. People may not believe it, but you're there to protect them."

"And so are you."

Emily smiled. "Yeah, I suppose, but in a different way." Her hand rested again on the butt of her gun.

"Why does every cop do that?" Hannah asked and pointed at her sister's hand on the gun.

Emily shrugged. "Security blanket, I guess, or just a comfortable resting spot. I guess it's kind of like an elbow on the center console in a car. Either way, it's good to know it's there. In my line of work, you never know when you might need it."

"That's so much truer today than ever with the anti-police sentiment going on."

"I don't worry too much about that. I have eyes in the back of my head, and I don't trust anyone."

"Yeah," Hannah said. "You've been like that since we were kids."

"A defense mechanism, I guess."

The girls fell into silence. Their eyes swept over the graves.

"Come on, let's get out of here."

"Yeah, it's time."

"We'll see you next week," Hannah said.

"We love you."

"Very much."

Together, Hannah and Emily left the grave site. A solemn silence moved the sisters close together, and arm-in-arm they walked toward their cars.

CHAPTER 6

orphanage

JAMIE ROCKWIN STILL felt disconnected from the world. The cold she had was wreaking havoc on her sinuses, which felt like a stopped-up sink. The medication she was on had succeeded in making her tired and did little to alleviate the symptoms. She felt worse today than yesterday, but her caseload was abundant, and the stack of files wouldn't go down if she remained in bed. There were so many voiceless children counting on her, whether they knew it or not. So up she got.

Upon arriving at work today she heard that yesterday, Paige, her boss, had Hannah handling one of Jamie's most fragile cases, and she needed to finish this one up so it didn't get dumped into her coworker's lap again.

It had been a battle with the mother of the young boy who was now sitting in Jamie's back seat. It had gone on for months. But it seemed no matter how many times she warned the stubborn, outright belligerent, and oftentimes aggressive woman that her son would be taken away if the living conditions didn't improve, during her random visits throughout the past weeks things would remain the same. Unchanged, without the slightest attempt at improvements. It was as if her warnings weren't being taken seriously, and this left her with no choice.

Jamie looked in the rearview mirror and saw the concern on the boy's face. She wished there was something she could say, but she knew he didn't trust or like her. In his eyes, she was the enemy; the one who took him away from his mother.

Regardless of his feelings toward her, today was a day of joy for Jamie, knowing that she would be delivering the child to a stable, structured household. It was a place where other children who were like him found refuge from the dysfunction of their families. They were given a reprieve from the chaos and a chance to see a different side of life. And that chance, although slim, may help them make better decisions as they grew into adulthood, she thought—and maybe it could keep them out of the system.

She was certain he would fit in quickly and be given an opportunity to have a normal life. He still had time. Time to embrace what was good and safe. Stay away from the drugs that were around him, learn responsibility, and maybe expand his education.

After Jamie dropped Urban off, she would need to go see Vicki and answer any questions she might have. She dreaded having to go there—that woman was so vicious, unclean, and mouthy—but it was how this worked. She would rather take the abuse than have the child endure it. Besides, there would be an officer present to make sure things didn't get out of hand.

Maybe now that Vicki had seen that the warnings she had been given weren't empty threats but had actual repercussions, she might be more amenable to talking to her rather than yelling at and threatening her the entire time.

Jamie pulled her vehicle into the driveway of a massive three-story house with about a dozen or so children playing in a side yard. Shouting and fits of laughter penetrated the vehicle and caught Urban's attention. He sat upright and watched, and Jamie looked at him in the rearview mirror.

"This is where you will be staying for a little while," Jamie said.

Urban didn't respond. He kept watching the children play.

Jamie watched them too. They varied in age and all seemed to get along very well. "Come, let's meet them," she said and kicked her door open. She opened Urban's door, and he grabbed his duffel bag and exited the car.

Jamie and Urban walked toward the group of children, and before they could reach them, a kind, pleasant-faced woman with a gentle smile emerged from the house.

"This must be Urban," she said.

"Urban, this is Joyce," Jamie said. "She runs the house here, and you're going to find out that her cooking is just as wonderful as her smile."

Urban turned away, disinterested.

"That's OK," Joyce said. "You'll like it here. At first, all the children that come here don't like it any more than you do right now. But after you meet everyone and see how they all get along, you'll settle in just fine. Come, let me introduce you to everyone."

Jamie nodded at Joyce, and she took Urban away. Jamie walked to her vehicle feeling a little bit better about taking the child out of his home. Now she needed to head back to the office to finish up some paperwork, then stop off at Vicki's. Jamie scrunched up her still-stuffy nose with dread. Going to see that woman was like having to walk the plank of a pirate ship.

"EVERYONE, I'D LIKE you to meet our newest member of the family," Joyce said. All the children stopped playing and walked over to where he and the lady stood, and formed a semicircle. "This is Urban."

"Hello, Urban," a small voice from the group said, and everyone followed with their greeting.

"He's tall," someone said.

These people were essentially faceless; they meant nothing to Urban. He didn't care about their stupid games and the pretty cut lawn and white picket fence or the big house next to him. He wanted to go home where his mother was and to where his father stopped by every now and then. The dilapidated house, dirt lawn, and the smell of cigarette smoke was good to him.

"Who would like to take Urban on a tour of the house?" Joyce asked. "Show him his room and where everything is? Give him the basic rules?"

Almost everyone raised their hand, and some of the smaller children stretched and tried to reach higher so they could be seen.

"Gwendolyn," Joyce said to the teen girl in the back who didn't even have her hand up. "Why don't you take Urban inside and show him around?"

All the other children grumbled in disappointment.

Gwendolyn was a pale, thin girl. Her long, straight, jet-black hair worked hard at covering the pimples on her cheeks. She wore black skinny jeans and a black t-shirt with a skull on it. Her fingernails were painted black, and when she stepped forward and walked past Urban, he could see she once had a nose ring.

"Come on," she said and walked with her head down. "Let's get this over with."

Urban followed her up the wooden steps that opened up to a porch with a swing on either side of the door. They entered the house, and Urban was taken aback by how clean and upscale everything was. A large semicircular couch and plush rug gave a comfortable feel to the large den, which had a flat-screen television that was so big it might as well have been a movie screen mounted on the wall. He had never seen a TV so big, with the exception of one at Wal-Mart.

There was a fireplace, and a humongous dining table with at least twenty chairs around it had a setting in front of each seat, and beyond that was the kitchen. Two ovens, two sinks, two refrigerators, and two dishwashers.

"So, this is how the rich live?"

"I suppose," Gwendolyn said, seemingly disinterested in having any conversation.

"This is the first time I've ever seen anything like this." Urban folded his arms. "I'm not impressed."

"You're not here to be impressed. You're here to conform and be a functioning member of the household."

"Is that so?"

"We're required to clean up after ourselves, and the more you do the more you get," Gwendolyn said. "I'm still somewhat new here and learning how things go so I don't know why Joyce chose me to show you around."

"Maybe she wanted to show you how much you actually know. Or maybe that it's we're so close in age? Either way, at least you get a break from them, right?"

Gwendolyn stopped and looked at Urban. "Yeah, sure. They're just little kids, you know."

"Annoying I bet."

"No less than you. After the meals are served, we all pitch in and clean up and set things the way you see so we're always organized and ready for the next meal. With all these people living together under the same roof, it's important we clean up after ourselves."

"You already said that."

"Yeah, I suppose I did, but at least you can't tell Joyce I didn't tell you."

"I'm not the telling type."

"You will learn your role around here as we go along. You just kind of acclimate yourself into what's going on and find your groove. It's an easy place to live most of the time. Boring too."

Urban looked over his shoulder toward the door to make sure they were alone. "Do you like it here?"

"What are you a spy or something? Acting all secret and stuff. Are you making sure I'm not going to run away?"

"No, why, are you?"

"Don't be stupid. Who asks that question within the first five minutes of meeting someone?"

Urban shrugged. "I do, I guess."

"Well you shouldn't." Gwendolyn walked up the flight of stairs, her feet slamming into the wood planks like a sledgehammer.

"So, what's your story?" Urban asked, following closely, his eyes fixated on her round behind.

"What do you mean what's my story?"

They reached the top of the stairs, and Gwendolyn's eyes rounded with a deep-rooted anger, focused on Urban.

"Why are you so pissed off? I mean, I think you need to lighten up."

"And you need to keep your eyes off my ass and your opinions to yourself. You'll do much better here. I don't know who you are and what you're trying to get out of me, but everything is fine. You get me?"

"Yeah, I can see that."

Gwendolyn spun on her heels. "This level here is where the younger children stay. Two kids to a room, boys and girls always separated."

"Apparently not," Urban said.

Gwendolyn stopped. "What?"

"I mean we're not separated, and you're a girl and I'm a boy."

"I'm only showing you around. Relax yourself, would you? It's not like I'm gonna touch your pecker or anything."

"Maybe not today." Urban smiled.

"Yeah, maybe not ever. Don't be a dick. I can handle myself."

"Is that why you're here? Do you fight and get into a lot of trouble?"

"No, I don't fight and get into a lot of trouble." She went to the next flight of stairs. "I like to keep to myself, if that's OK with you? My business is my business, not yours. Stay out of mine, and I stay out of yours. People come and go here, so you can forget about us becoming friends."

"Yeah, sure, OK, whatever you'd like."

They reached the third floor. "This is where you'll be staying. Girls are on the right side of the hallway, boys on the left. Your room is the last door. Lucky for you the boy that was staying in there went back home so you have it to yourself."

"Cool."

"Put your bag in there and then come back outside. I'll introduce you to everyone. Oh, underneath each bed is a ladder in case of a fire. You open the window, hook the ladder around the sill, and drop it. It will unravel and get you out of here."

"Don't give me any ideas."

"What?"

"Fire. I don't care about them or this place. I just want to go home. If burning this place down—"

"Seriously, is there something wrong with you?"

"What?"

"You actually just said you're going to burn the house down!"

"I never actually said I was going to do it."

"Maybe I'm the spy and I tell Joyce that."

Urban shrugged. "Go ahead, see what I care."

"Don't be an asshole. Most everyone wants to go back home, but that's not gonna happen. And I'd appreciate it if you didn't do anything stupid. None of us asked to be here."

"So, you like it here?"

"There are worse places to be. It's better than home. I hate my parents. Abusive assholes that care more about their drug habits and dirtbag friends than they do about me. I guess I'd rather be here."

"That's sad."

"Yeah, oh boo-hoo. Let the world feel sorry for me because my parents are fuck-ups."

"Seriously, what's your problem?"

"You. Me. Joyce. Life. Take your pick."

"I'm not here to make enemies."

"And I'm not here to make friends. Now you'll know to leave me alone."

"You couldn't possibly have any friends with the way you are."

"The way I am keeps people at arm's distance. It's a great place to keep them so you don't get hurt."

"No wonder why you're dressed in all black," Urban mumbled.

"What's that supposed to mean?"

"You're as depressing as hell. Like you're going to a funeral or something."

"Shut up."

"You're a shitty guide."

"And you're a shitty addition to the household."

"Good. I like that. Maybe I can be a pain in your ass. The thing that you hate getting up to see every day. Maybe it'll inspire you to go back home."

"You already are, but you couldn't get me to go back home if you tried."

"So why don't you shut up and show me the rest of the stupid things I need to know about this place?"

"Jerk."

"Moron."

"Asshole."

"Jerk off."

"Hen lick."

"What the hell is a hen lick?"

She laughed. "I have no idea." She turned away.

Urban laughed. "That felt good, and look, I made you laugh."

"Don't flatter yourself. Now go and put your bag in your room."

CHAPTER 7

surprise

HANNAH LOOKED AROUND the small, second-story apartment for her car keys. "Trent, did you see where I put my keys?"

"Yeah," he shouted from inside the bedroom.

"I'm losing my mind. I'm putting things down, and I can't remember a minute later what I did with them."

Trent came out of the bedroom with the keys dangling from his fingers.

"On the bed?"

"On the sink. When you forgot to put on your eyeliner or whatever, you must've had them in your hand and set them down. I should've played hot and cold with you. That would've been entertaining."

"If you'd have made me late for work, I would've killed you." She smiled at him and raised a brow. "As gently as I could."

"Freak. I know what hides behind that smile."

Yeah, sadness that's kept hidden deep down inside, she thought. That part she would never show. "And yet I can remain amazingly organized at work, and do it while I'm juggling a million different things," she said. "But keys? Forget it. They teleport all around the house."

He kissed her. "That's because you don't have anyone grading you here, looking over your shoulder, and judging you every step of the way. Giving you a review and telling you how close you were to getting that raise, but you fell just a tad short and need to do a little extra. You know, over the extra you already do."

"Over a barrel."

"With something very big in their hands to shove it some place." He kissed her again.

"You're adorable and good to me," she said and stood on her toes to kiss his face.

"Thank you, honey. That was sweet. You all up on your toes and everything."

"Jerk." She jingled her keys. "Thank you. I've got to go. I've got a ton of things to do today."

"Yeah, well having so many dysfunctional people in the world will keep you busy forever. How do you eat an elephant?"

"One bite at a time, sweetheart. One bite at a time."

"Right!"

"They're not bad people," she said. "They're just running into some issues they need to work through."

Trent turned on his heels. "That's what I love about you. You always see the positive even when you're surrounded by so many negatives."

Hannah departed with a smile, hurried down the steps and out the door, but stopped at what she saw. The keys dropped out of her hand as she staggered backward, tripping on the bottom step and falling onto her rear.

Positioned in front of the door and purposely facing her was a wheelchair with a dummy sitting in it. The head was tilted at an odd angle, and drawn with magic marker was a poorly composed face of a man in distress. The mouth was pulled down in sadness, and the eyes had teardrops underneath them. On the shirt, the word 'daddy' was scribbled with haphazard strokes from the same marker.

Hannah sat and stared; the tears came hard, and so did the shakes. She looked down the street both ways but didn't see anyone or anything out of the ordinary. Her cell phone felt like a brick when she pulled it out of her pocket. Confusion whirled around inside her head as she tried to operate the touch screen with her clumsy fingers. The phone slipped out of her hand and clattered onto the cement between her feet. She searched for it as her eyes remained locked on the mannequin.

She remembered the night she'd approached her father when he was in the wheelchair. It was impossible for a five-year-old child to comprehend what "paralyzed" meant. "Brain damage" was as foreign to her as advanced trigonometry. When she shook her father and begged him to wake up, he just wobbled and drooled.

That vision was something she often struggled to keep out of her mind. And now this abomination that sat before her was almost an exact replica of the worst moment in her life.

Finding the phone, she somehow navigated around the cracked screen well enough to dial her sister.

"Emily?" Hannah breathed into the phone. Her hand quivered. "You need to come over quick."

She hung up the phone and continued to stare at the thing that silently mocked her and insulted the memory of her father. Her body felt like it weighed a thousand pounds and was filled with immeasurable sadness. Sadness so profound that it needed to stay down, because if she released it, she might not ever find calm in her mind again.

Maybe she should call Trent and have him come down. Yeah, she thought, that's what she was going to do. She tapped on his name, and he picked up on the second ring.

"I need you to come downstairs. Now."

She hung up, her stare fixated. Her calls for help now complete, there was nothing in the world other than her and the dummy.

CHAPTER 8

outrage

"DID YOU TOUCH it?" Emily said.

"I couldn't get myself to even if I wanted," Hannah said. She remained on the stoop with Trent's comforting arms wrapped around her.

Her sister paced, incensed.

"Neither did Trent," Hannah said, staring blankly. "We know better than that."

Emily pressed the button on the radio clipped to the shoulder of her uniform. She requested forensics and backup as she circled the dummy in the wheelchair. She paused and studied the jagged work of the magic marker.

"Don't even look at it," she told Hannah.

"I'm trying not to, but I can't unsee it—even when I close my eyes."

"The Sinners did this."

"The gang that killed all those people after your dad's accident?" Trent asked, rubbing slow, gentle circles on Hannah's back.

"Yeah, them bastards. The SS was spray-painted on the back of the chair." Her gloved fingers traced the letters. "I knew it. They're on the rise again, opening old wounds."

"Why?" Trent asked.

"Because that's who they are. What they do."

"You're telling me that they've targeted me?" Hannah interjected.

"I don't want to scare you, but I have no doubt they did." Emily looked at her sister. "Who else would do this? And with this tag? They're sending a message. Firing a shot across the bow."

Hannah stood. "I don't know why, but please, Emily, don't tangle yourself up with them over this."

Anger twisted Emily's face into something awful. "They do this to you . . . to Dad, Mom, Uncle Glenn, and Aunt Stefanie, and I'm supposed to turn away from it? I don't think so, Hannah, that's not how the law operates."

Hannah reached out to touch her sister, but Emily pulled away.

"Don't you remember what happened to Uncle Glenn when he retaliated out of anger?"

Emily ignored the question. It didn't require a response.

"Have you spoken to anyone lately who you think could have done this?"

"Someone that would know about Dad and what happened to him?" Hannah shook her head. "No. No one I can think of. It has been so long since that happened. I mean to Dad."

"Did anyone threaten you within the past few weeks? Maybe more recently than that?"

"I get threatened all the time," Hannah said. "It's part of my job. I mean, look at what I do."

"Stop," Emily said and slapped her thigh. "Think, Hannah."

"Take it easy, Emily," Trent said. "She's been through a lot."

"Shut up, Trent." She pounded her temple with her finger. "Go through it in your mind. Viable threat, who is it?"

Hannah shrugged and sank into thought. "I was working a case for a coworker of mine and picked up a kid named Urban Daraio yesterday," she said. "His mother's name is Vicki. She threatened me. She had real crazy eyes, but I didn't think much of it after we got the kid out of there. People act like that all the time. She's nothing special."

"Maybe, maybe not. What did she say?"

"She cursed me out."

"No Hannah, you're not listening. There is something in there. What did she say?"

"She read my name tag out loud. Told me she would remember me."

"There we go. That's a starting point." Emily took a notepad out of her breast pocket and wrote the names down. "Now you're going to have to have eyes in the back of your head. That goes for the both of you. Do you understand me?"

"I'm going to take the day off, and so will she," Trent said. "I'll keep watch over her."

"No," Hannah said and shrugged off Trent's embrace. "I'm not going to let them scare me into hiding. There are children relying on me."

"Trent's right, and I'm going to buck you on this," Emily said. "You should take the day. You seem very shaken up over this whole thing, and for good reason. Give yourself a day."

"Of course I'm shaken up," Hannah said. "You are too, but you put on this tough girl super cop act! And neither one of you are going to tell me what I can and cannot do! I'm not cowering to some thugs that are trying to use scare tactics against me. I'll let the police do their work—trust in you and your colleagues—and I'll continue to do mine."

"That's fine," Emily said and studied the names of the woman and child, committing them to memory just like Vicki said she'd do with Hannah's. "You just have to wait here until the other officers arrive so you can give them your statement. I'll check in with you in a little while. Make sure you answer your phone. I want to see who is connected with this Urban Daraio and Vicki, and at the very least, I'll pay her a visit. I'm going to shake the tree a bit and see who or what falls out."

CHAPTER 9

a mole

THE WEIGHT OF the cell phone in Urban's hand was only a fraction of the satisfaction it gave him. His huge smile made his amazement obvious. "So, how did you get this?"

"I have my ways."

"We all do, don't we?"

Gwendolyn nodded; her black hair starkly contrasted her white skin. "We can be resourceful when we need to be, I suppose. Even if we don't have a plan for it at the time."

"Oh yeah? Tell me what else you've got."

Gwendolyn went into her room, and Urban followed.

"Don't come inside," Gwendolyn said and extended a hand, keeping him out of the room. "If Joyce sees you in here it'll be all over for you and me. They'll ship you out within an hour, and probably send me somewhere else. Trust me. Boys don't go into the girls' rooms, and the girls don't go into the boys' rooms. Don't ever break that rule. Ever. Just keep watch while I get what I have to show you."

Urban folded his arms and watched the staircase, listening for anyone who might approach. He was distracted by the noise of Gwendolyn rummaging through what sounded like drawers or furniture being shifted. He shifted his focus to her instead of playing lookout, in case he needed to get back in there and take whatever it was she had to show him. At least it would give him an idea of where to look.

"Here," she said and came out of the bedroom holding an envelope.

"What is it?"

"A letter I found. Joyce left it on the table one night. I took it and hid it. She's very careful and well-organized, and I can't believe she didn't shake everyone down trying to find it. But I guess it was unimportant or she just forgot about it. Either that or she thought she shredded it. She shreds everything."

Urban took the letter and saw that it was still sealed. He twirled it in his hand.

"I don't get it. What am I supposed to with this?"

Gwendolyn sighed. "I'm thinking about calling you a dumb shit, but I don't want to start that crap again. Look with your eyes instead of your mouth. Seriously, hello? It has the address of this house on it. Whoever you're planning on calling needs to know where you are, don't they?"

Urban's face brightened. "Holy shit, you're a genius."

"Yeah, I think I just gave you the golden ticket out of here."

"I could hug you."

"No, thank you. I'd rather a frog do that. Haven't you noticed they haven't told you where you are?"

"No. I didn't even think about that."

"They do that, distract you while you're driving over here so that you don't have any leverage. They do it without your even knowing it. It's to keep you from running . . . maybe even from doing what you're about to do. So now you don't have to wonder where you are because you have it right there in your hand."

Urban looked at the address, and his smile grew. "I'm gonna make a phone call. Please keep a lookout for me. I'll make this quick and explain what's happening as soon as I hang up."

"OK," Gwendolyn said.

Urban dialed his mother's phone, and she picked up after the third ring. "Hello?"

"Mom?"

"Urban! Oh my God, son, where are you?"

"I'm staying at this orphanage house or something at 242 Stephen Street in a town called Bellmore. Do you know where that is? Can you send Dad to come and get me?"

"They have you in the rich area. You know I'm not going to let them keep you from me. Hang on tight. I'm calling your father, and we're going to come and get you, baby."

"OK, Mom. Hurry. I don't like it here, and I don't like being away from you."

"I don't know how you did it, but you're resourceful like your father, Urban. This was the best phone call you've ever made. Be ready to move at a moment's notice."

"There's this girl here that's helping me. We didn't like each other at first, but now we're cool. I want her to come with us. Her parents are bad, and she doesn't want to go back to them, but she doesn't want to stay here either."

"That's fine, baby. We'll be there in a little while. Hang up the phone and act like nothing is going on. But like I said, be ready to go."

"I'm ready, Mom. We're ready. I miss you."

He hung up the phone and gave it to Gwendolyn. She powered the phone down and took the letter back from Urban. "Did you reach whoever you needed to get in touch with?"

"Yes, I did, and they're coming for me," Urban said. "And I want you to come with me. Mom said it was OK."

"Joyce isn't going to let you go with them. She's going to call the police, and whoever is coming for you is going to get arrested for trespassing, child endangerment, and a bunch of other stuff. At least that's what I heard her telling some other kid that said he knew where he was and how to contact his father."

"They can't touch my father." Urban puffed his chest with pride. "He's a pretty bad man when he needs to be. You'll see. And if you come with me you won't have to worry about being moved from place to place because people don't think you fit in or whatever. You'll be welcomed by my family. And protected too."

Gwendolyn smiled. "I'd like that."

"I need you to listen. When they come, they come big. So we've got to be ready to go and move fast. Faster than you've ever moved before. Whatever you have here is going to have to stay. We won't have time to get our stuff."

"OK, we won't even try."

"You won't even try what?" Joyce asked from the bottom of the stairs. Urban and Gwendolyn looked down at her. Gwendolyn hid the phone and the envelope behind her back.

41

"We won't even try to deviate from the rules," Gwendolyn said, and Urban slyly took what she held behind her back. Joyce looked down at her feet as she started up the staircase, and Urban hurried the items into Gwendolyn's bedroom and hid them underneath her pillow. He dashed back into place next to Gwendolyn just as he heard her finish: "Because they are there to put some stability back into our lives and create a sense of normalcy we've all been missing."

"Very good," Joyce said with a big smile. She stopped three quarters of the way up when Urban appeared. "You remembered our conversation from the other day," she said to Gwendolyn.

"I did," Gwendolyn replied. "Every word of it, and it makes sense."

Her smile faded. "Is the tour all done?"

"Yes, I showed him the house and told him what he needs to know. I even remembered to tell him about the emergency ladders under all the beds."

"Very good. So, what do you think, Urban?"

"Just put my backpack into the room. I like it. I think it's much better than where I was. I'm sorry if I came across as a jerk before."

"Thank you, and I'm really glad to hear that. Come on outside so we can introduce the newest member of our family without being so formal. Maybe you can get in on the game, Urban. What do you think?"

"I'd like that," Urban said and started down the steps. Gwendolyn followed closely behind.

"What about you, Gwendolyn?"

"You know me. I'm not interested in that sort of thing."

"You'll give in one day and realize how much fun you've been missing out on."

"Maybe, but I doubt it."

CHAPTER 10

a hunch

EMILY RUMMAGED THROUGH the precinct's computer database, with a huge stack of case files next to her and papers scattered across her desk in some sort of chaotic order only she understood. She glanced at the papers, shuffled them around some, and then looked again at the computer screen. She sat back, deep in thought, the buzz throughout the precinct merely background noise. No matter how deeply or where she looked, the connection was lost on her. Still, her suspicion had been raised, and it kept her sniffing like a bloodhound.

She pushed the chair back, stood, went to the captain's office, and knocked on the closed door. He motioned her in.

"Hey, Captain."

"How's your sister?"

"Shaken up pretty bad when I left. I haven't spoken to her since."

"Maybe you should check in, see how she's doin'?"

"I will. But there's something more pressing."

"And you? How are you holding up?"

"Right now, there's something I need to talk to you about. I'm going on a hunch here, so bear with me."

The captain pushed his glasses onto the bridge of his nose and rested his elbows on the desk. He looked at Emily, giving her his undivided attention.

"You know about the reemergence of the Sinners. Oddly, or not so oddly, it was that gang that was responsible for the death of my parents and uncle."

"I remember it well," Captain Creighton said. The subject was still an open wound to most. He kept his tone soft, but the hurt was impossible to hide. "I was a uniform like you at the time. The town was scared, but they rallied behind your uncle during the trial. It was a time of terrible crisis and yet a show of solidarity and strength against something evil and oppressive."

"I just read the case files. All of them."

The captain sat back and interlaced his fingers. He pursed his lips and gently rocked in his chair.

"I never asked you a thing about what happened. Beyond the little bit that I know from memory or what I had picked up along the way from my aunt or chatter from people is—"

"What is it, Emily?"

"I don't know." She submitted to silence. "Hannah, my sister . . . she removed a child from this home yesterday. The mother, Vicki Daraio, she read Hannah's name tag and told her she wouldn't forget it. She threatened her."

"Do you want to go and talk to this Vicki Daraio?"

"I most certainly do. Somehow, I feel she is connected to the Sinners. She has an arrest record for assault, drugs, theft, and parole violations. All of that stopped after she had the kid."

"OK," Captain Creighton said. He stopped rocking and watched her in silence.

Emily's expression changed. "This child, Urban; she doesn't make mention of who the father is."

The captain nodded, an indication he was following her. He was relaxed and patient, allowing Emily to complete her thought.

"Maybe I can go there. Bring up her affiliation with the gang. How they've begun to increase their activity in the town again. It so happens that my sister was targeted after Vicki made a threat."

Captain Creighton hesitated. He pulled the chair forward, picked up the radio, turned up the volume, and pushed the button.

"Frerk, come in."

"I can go alone, Captain."

He shook his head, held up a hand. "You could, but you won't."

"Go ahead, Captain," Frerk's voice crackled through the radio.

"Switch to five." The captain turned some buttons.

"I'm on five," Frerk said.

"You in?"

"I'm on my way in now."

"Come to my office. We have something cooking here that smells, and I need you to help Emily sniff it out."

"10-4."

The captain fiddled with the buttons again.

"Shake her hard. Let her know we know the kid your sister took out of the house is Beto's son."

"You remember his name?"

Captain Creighton sighed. "Anyone that was a part of the police force at that time could never forget it."

"Where has he been?"

"Probably in a rabbit hole. Maybe he left town for a while and came back—I don't know. We suspended the search for him over fifteen years ago. We figured the gang had been dismantled for good and he had fled. He'd become a ghost."

"How did you know I was suspecting this Beto—even though I didn't know his name—might be responsible for the wheelchair incident?"

"It's the only thing that makes sense. It's logical. He was the only one left standing that would have that information. They were a bunch of punks, not record keepers. The thought crossed my mind while I was watching you sift through those files on your desk. I tried to dismiss it and wanted to see what you came up with without my interference."

Frerk knocked and then came in. He closed the door behind himself, clapped Emily's shoulder, and sat next to her. "Sorry about your sister. I'm sorry about what was done. Them messing around in something so painful makes me want to hurt them. Those assholes are going to pay."

"That's why you're here," Creighton said. "You're going to be taking a ride with Emily. You're going to Vicki Daraio's house. Let Emily shake her down and put some real pressure on her. Let's see if we can get that canary to sing."

"OK."

"Did you get anything from her yesterday?"

"Beyond that she's a super bitch and a terrible mother?"

"Yes."

"She read Hannah's name tag and repeated her name. It was like she was committing it to memory, now that I think about it. It was like she was doing that to be able to pass the information along."

"We know she did, and there's a connection there," the captain said. "Emily will inform you of what she knows along the way. Now go, and both of you, be safe and take care of each other."

"Always," Frerk said.

The two officers stood.

"Oh, Captain?" Emily said and took a pen off his desk with a scrap piece of paper. She wrote down a phone number. "Call my sister for me, if you would. Find out where they took that kid, Urban, and send a few units over there. I have a feeling this wheelchair dummy move was not only a message, but a diversion. The things they did back then . . . they were violent, but they weren't stupid. And it seems they're always on the move."

The captain picked up the radio, and Emily and Frerk exited the office.

"We'll take my car," Frerk said. "I know right where this bitch lives."

CHAPTER 11

body bag

TRENT RAN TAUT fingers through his hair with the imagery of the dummy in the wheelchair running through his mind. Hannah shaking in his arms, whimpering at the thing. No matter how tough she tried to be, she was a mess. Broken, too, but unwilling to acknowledge that.

The thing he'd seen had replicated what Hannah described that one time she had opened up to him. They had been having dinner. Candlelight, soft music playing in the background, and the chandelier was turned low. She looked at everything around her and then her face reddened, obvious even in the dull light. The tears that streaked her face were her soul bleeding. The uncontrollable shaking was her heart still breaking, and the deep, throaty moaning was her essence calling out for a reason to the chaos she had witnessed. She told him what she saw her father become and how it haunted her every day.

Something inside her was fragmented and had been left that way for so long it was beyond repair. But she did a great job of hiding it, fooling everyone around her. Oftentimes he thought to ask her about it, to get her to talk about it so that she could mourn, but he always decided against it. Being stuck between wanting to help but also not wanting to cross the line had become tiring. He was in an endless state of indecision. But deep down inside he knew he had no place trying to break into the fortress of pain she kept so heavily guarded until she decided to let him in once again.

But the Sinners had created that place so long ago, and now they'd returned by leaving that dummy outside their door. It was a mockery of her father. A battering ram to her fortress.

He slapped the shower wall.

"I'll kill those bastards if they show their faces around here, I swear to God!"

The flash of anger eroded, and he lowered his head under the powerful spray of the showerhead. His hands worked his scalp aggressively and pushed around the soap as he attempted to mop away the thoughts that raced through his troubled mind.

Hannah should have taken the day off. He made that abundantly clear, but she wasn't having any part of it, and like attempting to get her to talk about what happened, he knew not to push her when she said no. She was firm in her stance. Firm in her reasoning. He couldn't blame her, because this so-called gang—these Southside Sinners—had taken so much from her, and she wasn't willing to give them any more. Christ, they had taken from him now too. This was what she referred to when she spoke about things snowballing out of control. It was a tangible feeling.

"They've already stolen from me. Taken things I can never get back," she had said after the police had left that morning. "I will not give them any more of myself. I am stronger than this."

Then she had kissed him and walked out the door. Trent stood there and watched her leave; the wet spot the kiss left behind almost stung. There seemed to be a finality about it. He was powerless in all of this. He couldn't do anything to help her, and if he was being honest with himself, a part of his own anger was that he felt emasculated. These Sinners were an intrusion, a cancer, and they had hurt the one person he would do anything for.

Anything, he thought.

He turned off the shower, dried his body, wiped away the fog on the mirror, and stared. His anger had turned the whites of his eyes red.

"One minute alone with one of them is all I would need." He spoke loudly and slapped the counter. "One minute!"

He seethed, breathed heavy. He threw some jabs and a hook punch, feinting left and right and following with another barrage of punches that were sloppy and weak, but damaging and unstoppable to his reflection.

"Pow! It'd be over just like that." He stood upright and tried to catch his breath. "Damn bunch of cowards, that's what they are!"

Giving into his anger was tiring, so he sat on the toilet seat lid and dressed. He brushed his hair, unsure if he'd be able to concentrate at work today. He just couldn't shake the image of seeing Hannah like that. A sound from the bedroom drew his attention.

"Hey, hun, are you OK?" Trent called out. "Did you think it through and decide to take the day?" He cracked the door open to make it easier for her to hear him and he her. Cool air rushed inside the still-steamy bathroom. He put a dab of toothpaste onto his toothbrush and thought for a moment. "I'm glad. I'll call in too. We can spend some time together. Figure things out. Maybe we can go for a walk?"

The springs on the bed squealed. Whenever either one of them sat in that spot to put on or take off their shoes and socks, the bed would make that sound. It was unmistakable.

Trent stepped out of the bathroom and froze. He dropped his toothbrush, his lips covered with white foam. Standing there, wordlessly, his bravery quickly shrank into nothing and abandoned him for good. He swallowed what was in his mouth.

A large man looked back at him. He was, indeed, sitting on the edge of the bed. He smiled when he saw Trent, and stood. He had a bat in his hand, and he slung it over his shoulder.

Louisville Slugger.

The black embossed emblem was unmistakable. The malevolent stare the man had centered on him was like looking the devil in the face.

"I've been listening to you. It was all so very cute," the man said. "So confident in front of a mirror, talking shit. Well, here I am. Show me your 'pow,' and let's see what you can do."

Trent was cemented in his spot in the threshold between the bathroom and bedroom, the words he had spewed now bouncing around regretfully in his head. If he took them back—begged, even—would it make a difference? Maybe if he said he was just blowing off some steam he would somehow get a pardon?

But his mouth wouldn't open. The toothpaste had glued his lips together. He was stuck, frozen by fear.

"My name is Philly Pavone, but everyone calls me Bones. Philly's not my real name, but I'm kinda partial to that team. I was told I should try out, but I have to practice a bit more. I don't come cheap and I always get the job done."

Trent had never been in a physical altercation in his life, and if he knew someone was listening, he never would have said those words. Especially this guy.

"*Grande bocazas!*" the man shouted and lifted the bat off his shoulder.

Instinct made Trent raise his hands to shield himself as the big man approached, but mere flesh and bone were no match for the lumber and the forceful swing that crashed through his weak defenses. Trent's forearms shattered, and the end of the bat carried all the way to his jaw.

Crack!

Stars filled his head, and he staggered. His jaw dangled, broken from the blow. Blood spilled to the floor. His arms had no feeling, and bone poked through the skin as rough shards of white coated in red. In an odd thought, he conjured their likeness to Wolverine's claws.

Everything had slowed down for Trent the moment he saw the bat leave Bones' shoulder.

Bones.

Trent had seen the bat coming, but nothing felt real. It felt like a lifetime had passed, and he was reaching the end of his. He was now immersed in a dizzying moment coated with fear of what was yet to come.

He tried to plead for something but only managed a grunt. His tongue numb, his wherewithal had been pounded out of his head. He tried to raise his arms, but they dangled limply at his sides, and his hands had already begun to turn blue and maybe a little purple, too.

Philly "Bones" Pavone laughed and seemed to genuinely enjoy the suffering he had inflicted.

"Messages need to be sent. Fear instilled. I see yours, and I like it. If I would've known this was going to be so much fun, I wouldn't have charged them for this." He swung the bat again and again and pounded the wood into Trent's legs, arms, torso, back, and head.

Somehow, Trent had managed to stay upright. Confusion, pain, and the instinct to survive guided him. Involuntary screams helped him cope with the heavy, repeated thuds of the bat. His body trembled, and he could hardly manage a thought outside of the pain and inexplicable fear that was being beaten into him.

Blood painted the four walls and sprayed the ceiling. Everything was so red. And Trent associated the redness with his pain leaving his body as it was being broken into bits, leaving behind a strange numbness.

He saw one last swing come for the side of his head. It was a welcomed thing, this blow, to take away the pain and the fanciful reality that had gone astray. The wood connected with a bone-breaking crack and toppled him over. He fell backward into the bathtub, and his body tore down the shower curtain and rod, wrapping him up like a body bag.

CHAPTER 12

foster home

JOYCE SAT ON the porch swing and watched the children play. She paid special attention to Urban. Tall and slender for a thirteen-year-old, he laughed as he kicked the ball to the other children. He had a great smile and a contagious laugh. All of the younger children took to him immediately, and he seemed to be settling in nicely.

Joyce opened the folder on her lap. She read Jamie's report and viewed pictures of a house that was in shambles. Filth, food scraps, and drug paraphernalia presented a danger to the welfare of the child, and it tugged on Joyce's heart.

"Oh my," she whispered and continued to peruse the contents of the file. Another picture showed a back—not the child's—that was covered in bruises. What looked like cigarette burns blistered the skin, and scars were seemingly inflicted by the blade of a knife.

"Check this out!"

Joyce trembled as her attention was yanked from the picture. She looked as Urban kicked the ball hard. It slammed little David Walch in his face and knocked him down. David started to cry, and Joyce jumped to her feet and hurried to his side. David held his nose. Blood dripped and covered his shirt. Joyce helped him up.

"Come on," she said. "Let's get you cleaned up."

She looked at Urban, and he was smiling. He laughed when Joyce turned away and started for the house.

Urban opened his arms. "You're the one that wanted me to play with them. I guess you won't be asking me to do that again."

Joyce remained calm and spoke to the young ones. "Come along with me, children. We need to go inside now."

The kids groaned in protest.

"I don't want to hear any complaints," she said. "You too, Urban. I'll need to have a word with you inside."

Joyce walked into the house and tended to David. She turned and looked at the cute blonde-haired, blue-eyed girl named Jacqueline Casimano, who hovered nearby, always eager to help. "Jacqueline, can you go and get David an ice pack?"

"Yes, Mrs. Joyce," Jacqueline said.

"Thank you."

Joyce pinched David's nose and had him lean his head back as Jacqueline hurried off. "Did Urban come in yet?" she asked the others.

"No, I think he stayed outside with Gwendolyn," Jacqueline said from inside the kitchen.

"Why doesn't everyone relax so I can have a talk with Urban? Jacqueline, can you please hold the ice to David's nose and watch over everyone?"

"Yes, Mrs. Joyce," the girl answered as she hurried back with the ice pack.

She was wise for a seven-year-old, with the natural instincts of a caregiver—something her biological mother didn't have. She was the child who had blossomed the most despite having come from one of the most horrific situations. Beatings, neglect, and sexual assault. The things in her file were so bad that Joyce didn't like thinking about it. It broke her heart and made her angry all at once. Every time she got another child and read the case file, she wondered how parents could be so cruel to their own.

All of the children went to the huge couch and one turned on the television. Joyce could confidently leave the room for a few moments, as the children were typically respectful of whomever she appointed as temporary leader.

Joyce felt apprehension as she turned away and approached the door. Urban was pure trouble, and he radiated anger. It had turned that quick. She looked through the screen, and her eyes settled on Urban, who was sitting with Gwendolyn, laughing.

Malice was his intent. It didn't take twenty years of experience to be able to spot that.

He was reenacting slamming the ball into David's face, using his hand to slap his own face and snapping his head back and sprawling himself flat in the grass. He sat up and acted like he was crying. His fists dug at his eyes.

Joyce stepped outside and walked toward Urban.

"I don't find what you did to be funny at all."

Urban looked up at her. "I really don't care what you think. I think it was hilarious."

"I think you owe him an apology. He's only five years old."

"I don't give a crap if he was two. I'm not apologizing to anyone. Why would I when I did it on purpose?"

"So, you want to spend your time in a detention center, locked up and told what to do twenty-four seven, rather than living in a place like this where you can learn basic coping skills and family structure and have freedoms?"

"Lady, I already know how to cope, and I was torn away from my family. That's something I can't cope with. Get me?"

"I get it. You're angry, but you don't need to take it out on a kid. David is a sweet boy that has had a tough upbringing."

"Doesn't matter to me. You ain't gonna get any sympathy from me. I take it out on whoever or whatever I like. He was there, so he was it."

Joyce looked down at him. "I looked through your file. I saw what you lived in, what you were exposed to. Those scars, bruises, and burns. Was that your mother or you?"

"Fuck off," Urban said. "You don't get to talk about what goes on inside my house, lady. And don't act like you give a shit either."

Joyce's eyes lit up. Never in all her years had she met someone this young so cold, so full of hate. He had a mouth so foul that it ruffled her normal calm and levelheaded thinking.

"What did you just say to me?"

"You heard me. I'm not going to repeat myself to you, so why don't you save your lecture for someone who gives a shit. I'll be out of here soon enough."

"Yes, you will with an attitude like that."

Urban held up his hand, acted like he was turning a crank on the side of it, and his middle finger slowly uncurled.

"Mrs. Joyce?"

Joyce turned around and saw little Mike Fulton holding up the telephone.

"There's someone on the phone that needs to speak with you. They said it was an emergency."

"I'll be making a call to get you out of here," Joyce said and turned away. She made her way up the steps and messed Mike's hair. "Thank you. You are a good helper."

"You're welcome, Mrs. Joyce."

Joyce took the phone, and Mike hurried away. "Hello?"

"This is Officer Eddie Powers," the deep-voiced officer said. His authoritative tone made Joyce pay attention. "We have reason to believe you and the children are in grave danger from a reemerging street gang that is related to one of the children under your care."

"Wait, hold on, what are you talking about?" she said but had a sinking feeling she already knew.

"His name is Urban. His father is the head of a ruthless street gang, and we believe they are on their way to your place to try and take him back. They will not hesitate to use extreme force."

"Oh my God." Joyce stared at Urban through the screen, and he was still carrying on with Gwendolyn.

"Get everyone inside, and don't answer the door unless you hear from me."

"Everyone is already inside except Urban and one of the girls," Joyce said. "He's being defiant. She's with him now, I think."

"He must know something is up. Hang tight. We're on our way."

Joyce opened the door and saw a beat-up vehicle creeping down the street. "Urban! Gwendolyn! I need you two to come inside right now!"

Gwendolyn laughed, and Urban put his arm around her shoulders.

"I'm not playing around with you two. Get inside of this house right now!"

"Yeah, sure," Urban said over his shoulder. "I'll get right on that."

Joyce looked in the other direction, and the street was empty. The creeping car sped up, and she saw men pointing at her house. The darkness within the car concealed mostly everything, but she could clearly make out guns.

"They're here, and they have guns!"

The vehicle rolled to a stop in front of the house, and the men piled out. Despite being the middle of the afternoon, they made no attempt to hide what they were doing. They checked their guns by pulling on levers, and Joyce couldn't believe what she was seeing. The roar of engines and the squeal of tires came from the other direction as two cop cars came to intercept the gun-wielding men. Their vehicles spun sideways, and four officers spilled out of their squad cars and into the street. They used their vehicles as shields and drew their weapons. This was going to be bad. Joyce retreated into the house with a slam of the door.

"PUT YOUR WEAPONS down, and get facedown on the pavement!" Officer Chris Press shouted.

The gang members, six in total, hid behind their own vehicle and opened fire as they scrambled for cover. The gunfire sounded like a jack-hammer. The street broke out into a war zone. Battleground had come back to Bellmore.

Urban stood, took Gwendolyn by the hand, and tried to pull her out of the yard and toward the car that had come to take them away. She pulled back.

"Let go of me!"

"What are you doing?" he said. "We need to get to that car! This is our only chance."

"They're having a damn shootout! You can't be serious if you think we have a chance of making it through the middle of that!"

"The police aren't going to shoot back if they see kids in the middle of it!"

"We are not going out there!"

Urban ran to a place where he could see better. "If an opportunity presents itself, I'm getting to that car, with or without you."

"Fine with me. I didn't want to think you were like everyone else, but you just proved you are."

"What are you talking about?"

"Just like everyone else does, you're going to leave me."

DANIEL MAXWELL, A large, hulking officer with limitless bravery, took aim down his sights and unloaded an entire clip into the car, pinning the gang down. Officer Press followed Maxwell's lead and unleashed a hail of gunfire.

Maxwell screamed out and fell to the ground; his gun dangled from a hand coated with blood. The blood dripped to the ground, dotting the pavement all around him. But Maxwell switched hands, reloaded, and climbed to his feet. He shot again, this time firing with more precision.

The pistols were hardly a match for the automatic weapons the gang was unloading, spraying the police cruisers, forcing them to hunker down. The bullets penetrated the police car, flattened the tires, ricocheted off the engine block.

Eddie Powers and his partner, Christine Balzafiore, a rookie just out of the academy, hid behind the wheels of the vehicle. Powers popped up, triggered off several rounds, and squatted back down. Maxwell, Press, and Balzafiore followed, all taking turns, random and accurate.

"Shots fired!" Balzafiore radioed in. "All available units, we need backup! 242 Stephen Street."

Officers Maxwell and Press exchanged gunfire with the gang members in an attempt to draw their gunfire. Their vehicle was pounded with a hail of bullets from automatic weapons, forcing them down again. Balzafiore stood, aimed, and took a single shot, hitting a gang member in the shoulder and dropping him.

As she ducked back down, she looked at her partner, and his sidearm was limp in his open hand at his side. Blood trickled from a bullet wound to the head.

"Powers!" she screamed and attempted to crawl to give him aid, but the bullets that skipped beneath the patrol car kept her in place.

"I have an officer down!" Balzafiore shouted into her radio. "Officer down, and one wounded! We're taking heavy gunfire from automatic weapons!"

Balzafiore popped up again and unloaded her entire clip into the vehicle with a distance of no farther than twenty-five yards. She screamed as she did so, adrenaline taking over. Maxwell and Press joined in on the hail of bullets their fellow officer rained down on the gang. This was their final stand, with ammunition running low and no backup coming for at least another several minutes.

The gang members shriveled out of sight, using their vehicle as cover. Officer Press dropped his clip and quickly reloaded. He continued to fire, employing the same tactic to skip bullets beneath the vehicle in hopes of catching one of the criminals in the ankle or leg.

THE BACK DOOR to the gang car opened, and Marie Brugger got into the driver's seat and sat low. Her fellow gang members had moved around the vehicle as she backed it up and turned it sideways. It was her boyfriend, Santiago, who had been shot.

"Get in," she shouted.

The gang piled into the car all the while taking gunfire. Marie went limp and blood pumped from her side.

"She's been hit!" Sandra Cuesta shouted. She yanked Marie's limp body into the passenger seat and got behind the wheel. She reversed down the street, skidded, and spun the car until it faced away from the officers. Sandra slammed the car into drive, and blue smoke from the screaming rubber filled the air as she turned the vehicle around the nearest corner and disappeared out of sight.

THE AWKWARD SOUND of silence followed what had been a cacophony of violence. As the other officers closed in on Officer Powers, Officer Maxwell went to the trunk of his vehicle, removed a raincoat, and placed it over the fallen officer. He sat next to him and cradled his own injury, applying pressure to help slow the bleeding.

Officer Balzafiore, in shock, wandered the street where the gang car had been, and she looked at the blood on the ground. Splashes here and there. Someone had been hit. By the amount of blood left behind, they might've hit two of them—hopefully more.

A child, red-faced with tears in his eyes, pushed Officer Balzafiore, sending her staggering.

"What the hell did you just do, you pig?"

The child came at her again, and Balzafiore tossed the kid to the ground. He landed in a smear of blood from one of the gang members.

"Get the hell off of me, you pig!" Urban shouted.

Balzafiore easily cuffed him, stood, and tried to assess exactly what had just happened. The venomous words continued to pour out of the child's mouth, but Balzafiore could hardly hear them over a constant ringing in her ears.

She had been in the middle of hell and had somehow come out unscathed. Officers Powers and Maxwell hadn't been so lucky.

The reality of what she had been through finally broke through, and adrenaline made her shake and feel a bit lightheaded. She needed to sit and found relief as she listened to the wail of approaching sirens.

"Are you OK?" Press asked.

"I'll be fine," Balzafiore said. She decided to lie down on the patch of grass between the sidewalk and street. That was a good place to be right now.

CHAPTER 13

sick day

PAIGE ROYALTY WATCHED Jamie Rockwin from her office. The glass office with shades had an eerie, heavy feel to it today, and Paige shivered because of it. It had become a glass cage. A fishbowl where she was exposed to everyone. Every little secret she had was in the open for everyone to see.

"Damn," she whispered and wished the skin she was in wasn't hers. She had come to realize that her aspiration was nothing more than a curse. To have worked so hard for so long and to have finally earned the title of boss had become meaningless. Comparable to one trying to build a sandcastle as the tide receded only to have it come sloshing back a few seconds later. Never in a million years did she think it would mean this. To become this.

Jamie was one of her hardest workers, had hardly ever missed a day, and always stayed a little later to help move the overabundance of child welfare cases along. Her belief in what she was doing, the help she was providing to the voiceless, and her compassion were the main drivers of her dedication and her prevailing attributes of being a good human being. She was kind, smart, funny, and most importantly, genuine. It seemed she shared the exact same misfortune as her boss but didn't realize it.

Paige reached a shaking hand out, turned the knob to her office door, and opened it. The bustle of the industrious office came crashing down on top of her. Busy people scurried about. Phones rang, printers hummed, and voices piled on top of one another, creating a chaotic cacophony of production.

Paige pulled her door closed behind her, walked over to Jamie's desk, and could barely look her in the eyes.

Jamie was busy organizing papers and a folder.

"How are you feeling?" Paige asked, the coming answer irrelevant. Her next moves were scripted.

Jamie paused and looked at her boss with glossy, reddened eyes, her nose bright like a beacon. "A little better than yesterday, I think."

"Did you get the child . . . what was his name?"

"Urban."

"Right, Urban. Did you take him to where he was assigned?"

"Without incident," Jamie said with a smile, hampered by her cold. Her voice sounded a bit masculine.

"I want you to take the rest of the day off."

Jamie paused and settled into a state of confusion. She looked at all the files piled on top of her desk and shook her head. "I have so much work to do. I can't just take the day off. I still have to drop by Urban's mother's house and deliver the final paperwork to her."

"I understand your dedication, and you know how much I appreciate it. But I don't need you getting everyone here sick. I've been watching you from my office, and no offense, you look like hell. You sound even worse. Your eyes are red and watering, and you have no color."

Jamie busied herself again. "Just let me deliver the papers to the Daraio woman and put this part of the case to rest. The psychologist can take it from there, and I can move onto the next case starting tomorrow."

"You're not listening, Jamie. I'll get someone else to deliver those papers. You're sick and shouldn't be here."

"Boss, I can do this. I need to do this after what happened with Hannah yesterday."

"I know you can, and I know how bad you feel, but I'm not permitting you." Paige moved closer. "I'm not asking. I'm telling you that your day is over."

"But it just started."

"Your day is over, Jamie. Stop working immediately. You have five minutes to get out and head home. Get some rest. It'll do you some good." Paige held out her hand. "The Daraio file. Give it to me. If it makes you feel any better, I'll handle it personally. I won't put anyone else in front of this woman."

Jamie reluctantly handed the file over.

"Thank you, and feel better. Don't think this is a punishment in any way. We have to look after each other. It's as simple as that."

Jamie nodded and took her purse out of the bottom drawer of her desk. She stood, slung the bag over her shoulder, and left the office.

From the security of her fishbowl, Paige watched Jamie leave. She closed the blinds, sat behind her desk, and picked up the phone she had left resting on her desktop.

"It's done. I sent her home."

"Good," said the strong male voice on the other end. "And the file?"

"I have it here in my hand."

"Shred it."

"OK," Paige said.

"Do it now. Let me hear it."

Paige ran the pages through the shredder until the file was empty.

"It's done."

"If you're trying to fool me . . ."

"I'm not. I've done everything exactly as you said."

"Well then you have nothing to worry about. That is, unless you tell someone about our conversation and about what you did. God help you and your family if you didn't destroy that case file or if you get caught."

"I won't say anything. I did as you said and destroyed the case file," Paige said and felt a heavy heart sinking farther into her chest. "My family is too important to me. Please, don't hurt them. I did as you said. Everything."

"I'll keep my word as long as you keep yours," the voice breathed into the phone, the threat it posed tangible. The fear it instilled left a lasting impression. "You can take comfort in the thought that you've kept your family safe from the Sinners. Employed in our protection is a big thing," said the uncaring voice. "Now be careful of a guilty conscience. Don't let it get ahold of you. If you let it, it can cost you and the people you love dearly. It can undo all the good you've done today. One little misstep is all it takes. Do you understand that?"

"Yes."

"Good."

The caller hung up the phone, and Paige did too. She sat at her desk, unable to move, the swirling sensation in her chest and her need to cry climbing up her throat, almost unable to be contained.

"I had to do it," she said to herself through the flow of tears. "I'm so sorry. I had no choice." She submitted to her emotions and collapsed into herself. "Believe me. I had no choice."

CHAPTER 14

getting to know each other

OFFICER FRERK EASED the police cruiser to the side of the road and parked in front of Vicki's house. Frerk and Emily exited the car, and Emily evaluated the condition of the house.

"What a shithole," she said, navigating the dilapidated walkway while she kept an eye on the front door and windows. Her hand rested on the butt of her gun, and Frerk remained at her side.

"Same thing your sister said to me." Frerk pounded his knuckles on the rusty screen door and stepped back. "I hope this lady remembered to put on actual clothes today. When Hannah and I were here yesterday, Vicki wore a shirt that was see-through. My eyes still hurt from seeing her saggy boobs."

Emily laughed, but it didn't lessen the tension.

Vicki answered the door, and her shoulders fell forward at the sight of the officers.

"What now?"

"Invite us in or come outside. Either way, we talk," Emily said.

"Yeah? What if I don't want to?"

Emily chuckled. "You don't have a choice."

"This is harassment," Vicki said and came outside. She looked Emily over with a hint of confusion.

Vicki's clothes were exactly as Frerk described: see-through and impossible not to notice her boobs hanging way down. A smell accompanied her and wafted out of the open door. Emily took a step back. It was the stink of stale, unclean air mixed with body odor, oozing out onto the stoop. "What is it?" the unpleasant woman demanded.

"I've been looking into your background," Emily said, "and it seems you have a tie to the Sinners."

"Had," Vicki said and crossed her arms. She leaned against the house, and it looked like she was assisting in holding it up. Either that or she was attempting to push it down on top of the officers.

Emily nodded. "Had. Yeah, sure. I get it. I'm to believe some two-bit dirtbag like you with a derelict kid. You lie, cheat, and steal. That's what bottom-feeders like you do. That's all you *can* do. That's the only way you know."

"That's real professional, Officer."

"So, tell me that again how you *had* ties with the Sinners. Are you sure about that? Be certain now in what you're telling me. You have no affiliation with the Sinners?"

Vicki glanced at Emily's name tag. "Oh, I see. You're here because I scared your little sister?"

"The looks give it away?" Emily fired back.

"Hah, I get it, twins." Vicki rolled her eyes. "As if I wasn't able to figure that one out the second I saw your smug face. You share that look, you know? It's a stupid look, if you're wondering. That and that dumb last name that's impossible to forget." She looked at Frerk then back at Emily. "Your sister is the one that took my son from me. She came here and took my son. How can I forget that?"

Emily looked around. "Nothing I see or smell here would give me a clue as to why."

"Up yours."

"I'm about to shove it up yours. You threatened her yesterday," Emily said and stared hard.

"I did no such thing."

"Now, Vicki?" Frerk said. "You're going to stand there and lie with a straight face when I was there and heard what you said?"

Vicki stared with her mouth hanging open. "When did I threaten her?"

"Telling her that you'd remember her last name is passive aggressive, and in light of what happened yesterday, I would be hard-pressed to say your words were a coincidence rather than a threat."

"I haven't made no threats, so it's like you said—a coincidence. Besides, I have no idea what happened."

"It just so happens when my sister woke up this morning and was leaving for work, she had a present outside her door from the Sinners. I'm sure you know the symbol. The 'SS' with the little devil tail at the end? It was a message, a reminder of what the club had done to our father all those years ago."

"I don't know what they do. I haven't been associated with the Sinners since Urban was born."

"Bad move."

"I didn't want Urban around that crap. The violence they show toward the women and the heavy drug use was something I didn't want him to see."

"And they let you go, just like that?" Frerk said. "C'mon, Vicki, we're not stupid. That's not how it works."

"After they raped and beat me, yeah. Fifteen men taking their turn from behind. Cutting my skin, putting their cigarettes out on my flesh while I was held down. I couldn't feel my face for a week, and my vagina bled for just as long. My back took so much longer to heal because I couldn't tend to it."

"A heavy price to pay. But what wouldn't a good mother do to protect her child?"

"I wanted out for my son, so in my mind, that was a small price to pay. Do you have a child?"

"I'm not here to discuss the dynamics of my family. I'm here to discuss yours and your affiliation with the Sinners."

"I told you I left them."

"But you have something that belongs to them, don't you? Something that makes it impossible to keep them away . . . to complete that separation?"

Vicki looked at her feet. "I don't know what you're talking about."

"I'm talking about his son."

"I have no idea where Beto is or what he's been up to. But I do know the piece of shit hasn't given me a damn dime to take care of Urban. I don't have two nickels to rub together, and that deadbeat is nowhere to be found."

"You see that?" Emily said and looked at Frerk. "I didn't even need to ask if he was the father because you know as well as I do she would've denied it, and we probably would've gone round and round in circles for a half hour before she gave in. But she knows we know. Just like I know that rape story is bullshit. Beto wouldn't allow anyone else to touch his old lady. The scars you speak about are from an ex or from Beto himself."

"So what? Yeah, fine, he's the father. What does that prove?"

"That you called him when my sister took your son, and your baby daddy had someone follow her to where she lives. Either that or he did it himself. I can write this shit. The script is easy to follow."

"How could I call him if I don't have his phone number?"

"Don't worry, Mrs. Dirty Leaning Against the Stinky House, I've already begun the process of subpoenaing your phone records. This is all very simple. I look forward to arresting you."

"Oh, so you're the bad cop?"

"Please resist arrest when I come to get you. You'll find out I'm as bad as they come. Your boyfriend is going to find that out too."

Vicki looked away and laughed. "Tough talk from such a small woman. Especially one that hides behind a badge."

"Talk that I can back up. You can pass that message along to the deadbeat dirtbag coward that he is. You can also tell him there is vengeance in my heart for what he did." Emily patted her sidearm. "This is something I'd like to shove up his ass."

Vicki shook her head. "You're not getting it. I'm not calling anybody. I'm working on cleaning up the house and myself so I can get Urban back. That's where my focus is. Beto hasn't been around. I don't care what you think."

"That sounded really convincing, but do you really think I believe that line of bullshit?"

"I don't care what you believe."

"I've been dealing with scum like you my entire career, and I've learned not to trust a single one of you. I'll be watching you, and when your dirtbag boyfriend shows up late at night and tries to crawl in through a back window, I'll be there to take him down."

"How many times do I have to tell you he doesn't come here, that I haven't heard from him?"

"Right," Emily said and turned and walked away.

"You've been given a million chances," Frerk said and followed Emily. "Now you have to live with what's coming. So brace yourself," he called over his shoulder.

"You should take your own advice," Vicki shot back, laughing as she slammed the door on the officers.

CHAPTER 15

radio

EMILY PLOPPED INTO the passenger seat, heaved a sigh, and let her head fall onto the headrest. Frerk slid behind the wheel, started the car, and pulled away, not saying a word.

Emily removed her phone and dialed out.

"Hannah?"

"Hey, Emily," Hannah breathed into the phone.

"How are you doing?"

"As good as expected. You?"

"No sense in fooling around here, so why don't I get right to the point."

"What are you talking about?"

"I made some connections, Hannah. I started to connect the dots, and I put the Southside Sinners right outside your door. They put that wheelchair and the dummy there."

"How can you know for sure?"

"It had to do with the kid. Urban. It was retaliation for him being removed from the mother's care. She's a Sinner, and the child is the son of one."

"Tell me this is all one big joke."

"I wish I could, but it seems as though you were pushed toward some shit and stepped right in it. You're not going to believe this, but Urban is the son of the one and only Beto."

The line went silent.

"I just confronted Vicki, and I think I have her scared," Emily said. "I don't think she'll so much as squeak out a fart because she's under the impression she's being watched."

"It wasn't my case. It wasn't my decision to remove the child from his home."

"I know, but they don't, and even if they do, they don't care. Fate has a funny way of putting things where they're supposed to be . . . or not supposed to be."

"Well, fate has a shitty sense of humor and I'm not laughing. The mother of that boy knows that her son being removed from that house wasn't my decision. She knows exactly who has been working on her case because she'd been dealing with her for months. We don't just trade off caseworkers."

"She plays dumb really well. The ID tag you wear has your last name, doesn't it?"

"Yes, it does. I'm required to wear it by the county. It's considered to be a part of my uniform."

"I'm not questioning why you wear it because that would be as silly as you questioning why I wear one with my badge. I was just stating how they were able to put together the pieces of who you are."

"This is absurd."

"Think about it. The daughter of a slain doctor, suicidal mother, and vengeful police officer that tore their gang to the ground removes the child from their home, and it so happens he's the son of the one person that eluded the police force for so long—a force on which the deceased's other daughter serves—the only original remaining member of the gang. There's no doubt she called Beto, and that's how he got your name. I'm speculating, but I have a strong suspicion he was acting in a retaliatory fashion."

"What does this mean? I've got to be honest, Em, I'm scared. I'm scared of the things you're telling me. Where is this going?"

"I hate to say it, but I think it means war. We're at war, and they're going to come with a show of force. I don't know when, but they will come. What they did to you was a prelude. Merely a message sent that they know who you are."

"Not this again, Emily. I don't want to go through this again! People are going to get hurt."

"Me neither, and yes, people are going to get hurt. But if I'm going to be a realist and take into consideration how these people act, I think confrontation is unavoidable at this point. Two trains are speeding toward each other on the same track. The brakes are out, and there's no conductor aboard. It's the passengers I'm worried about. I also think there's another reason they put that dummy in front of your place."

"What reason? What do they want?"

"To distract us. I think they're going to hit somewhere else. Do something really dramatic. Show how strong they really are."

"How strong are they?"

"We're unsure what they're capable of. They've been quiet for a long time. This is a reemergence, so we're going to have to wait and see."

"Aunt Stefanie—Mom?" Hannah breathed into the phone. "What about her?"

"I'm going to have the captain dispatch someone to her house if he hasn't already done so. I'm not too worried about her. I doubt they even know where she's living."

"And you, what are you going to do?"

"Get to work on this. Try and contain the collateral damage as much as possible."

"Emily?"

"I know. You don't need to say it."

Hannah remained quiet.

"Listen," Emily said. "Aunt Stefanie doesn't know this, so please don't say anything, but I looked into the case file. What these people did? I know everything, and they're vicious. She survived and witnessed the most awful things. They're violent beyond anything most people have ever seen."

"I'll have my head up and eyes open."

"At the very least you need to do that. I suggest you pick up pepper spray or something for now. I'll be giving you a gun."

"I'll get the Mace after work."

"OK."

The radio on the squad car buzzed to life.

"Shots fired! All available units, we need backup! 242 Stephen Street."

"I've got to go, Hannah. Things are going down."

"What sort of things, Emily?"

"A shootout. I'll call you later," she said as Frerk flipped on the siren and floored the cruiser.

"Be careful."

"As careful as I can be." Emily hung up the phone and exchanged looks with Frerk. There was an instant seriousness that clung to the officers. Life and death. The pivotal moment had come. The spark had lit the fuse. The feeling was palpable.

"It's like you said," Frerk said over the wailing siren. "War is breaking out again. I can feel things aren't right."

"Me too," Emily said.

"I have an officer down," a voice shouted into the radio. They were easily able to identify the voice as Officer Balzafiore. She was panicking. "Officer down, and one wounded! We're taking heavy gunfire from automatic weapons!"

FRERK AND EMILY rolled up on the aftermath of the shootout. The two squad cars were littered with bullet holes; glass and chunks of car were scattered about the street. Officer Balzafiore was on the lawn, seemingly unhurt but likely in shock. Officer Press was scouring the area.

A kid was lying in the middle of the street, shouting, his hands bound behind his back, his face red with rage, his clothes stained with blood.

Officer Maxwell bled from somewhere around his arm or shoulder. The deep blue uniform soaked with blood made it difficult to see exactly where. He sat next to the body of the fallen officer who leaned against the vehicle's front wheel. They had covered the body with a raincoat, but a substantial amount of blood had puddled up around it.

"Who is it?" Frerk said to Maxwell.

"Powers. It's Officer Powers."

"Shit. Was just talking to him this morning. He was going on vacation at the end of the week."

"They got him in the head. He's missing the right side of his face."

"Where are you shot?"

"My shoulder. They just missed my vest."

Emily watched the men in conversation, then broke away. She walked to the child in the middle of the street. He stopped his rant and looked at her with curled lips and exposed teeth. "This is all your fault! If you didn't take me away from my mom, this never would've happened!"

Emily knelt, grabbed Urban by his face, and squeezed. "Your mother caused this, and she should've gotten her shit together. Your father did this because he's a piece of shit, and you're going to follow right in his footsteps, aren't you?"

"Fuck you."

"Your mother," Emily said. "And your daddy, too. That's who I'm going to screw, you little bastard." She shoved his face away and stood. She spun where she was and saw that the devastation was long reaching. The blood, bullet casings, the dead officer, the wounded officer, the officer in shock . . . and her own bewilderment. The aftermath of war was everywhere.

She shivered.

"Battleground," she whispered. Why did this feel like it was only the beginning?

"He's going to get you for this!" Urban shouted. "Do you hear me, lady? He's going to get you and everyone you love!"

Emily wanted to kick the kid in his fat mouth but walked away instead. Her head filled with so many things that were happening at once. In this moment she didn't even know where her starting point was. She had little time to figure that out and act on it.

Tick-tock.

Every second felt like an eternity. But being forever in a state of confusion like this was torture.

CHAPTER 16

southside sinner

JAMIE COUGHED AS she took the keys out of her bag and sorted through the ring packed with gadgets and keys. She didn't know what half the keys belonged to but was certain of the one she was looking for. The pretty one with the sunflowers on it was for her front door.

She sneezed hard. "Ouch."

As much as she didn't want to admit it, it was probably best that Paige had sent her home. Her eyes burned, and an itchy, swirling feeling in her chest had only intensified over the last hour. It forced multiple fitful coughs that had resulted in a raw throat and a pressure headache.

Inserting the key into the knob, she twisted it and pushed the door open. Home sweet home. The medicine cabinet would be the first thing she'd be hitting once she got inside. After that, she'd plop down on the bed for a nice, long, drug-induced sleep. There would be no alarm; her cell phone would be turned off and her shades closed tightly, blocking out the sun and stifling the world beyond.

A forceful shove from behind caught her off guard. Her head snapped back, and her neck cracked. Air was forced from her lungs. She fell forward with tremendous force and reached her hands out to break her fall. Her purse went flying, and her arms gave way on impact. Her face skidded across the rough berber carpet. Pain, rugburn, and confusion left their mark. She motioned to roll to her back to see who or what did that, but sparks of discomfort made her hesitate.

The door slammed closed, and a heavy, crushing weight that kept the air from her lungs pressed down on her back. Her face mashed into the rug. Her lungs were on fire and tried to reset under the heavy weight. Her bones crunched, and her eyes felt like they were going to pop out of her head. She tried to speak but couldn't.

"No, no, it would be wise for you to stay down and keep quiet. Only speak when I ask you a question, and make sure your eyes stay down."

The gravelly voice of a man made her stiffen and forget her pain and cough. It seemed she could do without her breath for a while longer.

"You went to the wrong house and took the wrong kid," the man said. "Stupid move that's going to cost you dearly." The man clicked his tongue. "There is going to be a lesson in what you did. Don't fret though, because the lesson has already begun. I need to know, are you afraid?"

The man with the deep voice took some of the pressure off of her and allowed her to draw a breath. She gulped the air and coughed it out. She was helpless to do anything but follow his directions explicitly.

"Yes, I'm afraid," she managed to say. "I'm confused too."

The man laughed, and it made her skin goose.

"Good, you should be. How do you think a child feels when you take them from their home? Do you think the fear is similar to what you're experiencing right now?"

"I don't do it with malice," she groaned in protest.

"But you do it, nevertheless. Just like I'm going to do something to you. With no malice, but as a simple reminder. A reminder to consider other people and their feelings. A reminder that the profession you're in might not be the right one for you after this is done."

"Please," Jamie said.

Those words prompted the man to settle his weight on top of her again. She wheezed as the air slowly left her lungs. He grabbed her shirt and ripped it. He pulled it again and exposed her bare back.

He held a knife in front of her face, twirled it, and ran the dull side across her cheek.

"Now maybe you can understand the level of fear a child goes through when you rip them from their home. You break apart families," the man said and cut away her bra strap. "Because they have burdens you don't and couldn't possibly understand."

"I . . . try and . . . help . . . them . . ."

"No, you create hurt. The problem is you can't see that. Even with a knife to your face while you're pinned down and helpless. Maybe it's that you're just drunk with power. I don't know. Remember that for every action there is a reaction, and here's the reaction to what you've done."

The man pressed the blade deep into the flesh on her back. Jamie tried to scream but made no sound. She kicked and pounded the floor and clawed the carpet.

Her attacker dragged the knife in a jagged curve and held her down with his body weight. Blood poured out of the sliced flesh.

'SS'

The Southside Sinners logo had been forever engraved deep into her skin. A permanent reminder of this moment and of her decision to take Urban from his mother.

"That's payback, our reaction, a taste of what true power is. If you want to live, you'll keep your head down until I leave. You better learn to shut your mouth if you know what's good for you. Describe me, tell them what my voice sounded like, or how heavy I felt, and I will come back for you. Instead of your back, it will be your throat I slice."

The attacker got off of her and walked around the house for a moment. Jamie whimpered, clawed at the carpet, and bit back against the pain. She kept her head down, still feeling every cut the knife had left behind and how deeply the sharp blade went.

The back door slammed shut, and Jamie moaned. She was slow to raise her head to see if she was indeed alone.

Her purse was about ten feet away, the contents spilled in a trail that had followed her descent to the floor. She could see her cell phone and pulled herself along the rug. The pain was excruciating; the deep lacerations made it almost impossible to use her arms. Her back felt gaped open. *He must've cut into the muscle, too,* she thought. She got to the phone and dialed 911 with trembling hands.

"Please, send an ambulance. I've been attacked and stabbed. My attacker left, but there's blood all over the place, and I can hardly move. I feel like I'm going to pass out. Please, send someone quick."

Jamie let the phone drop out of her hand, leaving the call connected, glad she always kept location services on. She turned her head and rested it on the carpet, trying not to focus on the pain or what had been done to her in plain daylight.

She looked up and saw that, before the man left, he had wiped the knife off on her curtains, leaving behind disturbing imagery of what he had done and how much blood she lost. It was better if she closed her eyes and waited for rescue to come, Jamie decided. Besides, it hurt too much to move, nearly too much to even draw breath or blink her eyes.

CHAPTER 17

aftermath

HANNAH LOOKED DOWN the street both ways, certain no one had followed her or had been waiting for her. She had circled the block twice, even parked way back for a bit to watch, wait, and double-check. There was no odd activity, and nothing seemed out of place.

She hurried up the steps, readied the key to the front door, and slid it in the hole, twisting the tumblers and turning the handle. The door opened, and she put her keys away and stepped inside, locking the door behind her.

Clunk, clunk, clunk.

The sound came from the back of the house. She looked at the door she had locked and realized her escape would be severely delayed if she needed to flee. She unlocked the door and cracked it open so all that would be required was a pull. That would hardly be an obstacle to slow her down.

"Trent?"

Clunk, clunk, clunk.

The sound was strange, and her call to Trent only seemed to encourage the strange response. The zipper on her pocketbook was already pulled back, and she reached into the pouch and removed the pepper spray. Glad she listened to Emily, she stepped forward with the Mace leading the way. Each footfall touched the floor like a feather but somehow seemed to find the plank of wood that squealed the loudest beneath her weight. As she moved through the apartment, she noted that nothing was out of place and that it was eerily quiet outside the sound of her approach and that other unfamiliar sound.

Clunk, clunk, clunk.

There it was again. The impossibly unidentifiable sound beckoned her onward like a curled finger digging into the air.

"Trent, honey, what are you doing?" she called out as calmly as she could muster.

Still, there was no answer, and she'd reached the short hallway that dead-ended at their bedroom. The hair on the back of her neck and arms stood. She looked over her shoulder at the door and thought to make a speedy escape.

Clunk, clunk, clunk.

But that sound stole her attention and thoughts, somehow smothering her trepidation and twisting it into something of curiosity. That's not to say her fear hadn't remained—because it did—it just collided with the strong desire of needing to know. To know what she had been hearing and what was going on.

"Trent, if that's you, you're scaring me."

Clunk, clunk, clunk.

Hannah reached the doorway of the bedroom and saw blood spray all over the walls and a huge puddle in the threshold between the bathroom and bedroom. She dropped her hand to her side, and the pepper spray fell out of her grasp. It thumped dully at her feet. Her mind worked overtime to try to piece together what she was looking at. Carnage. That was the only word that came to mind. Was it even real?

Clunk, clunk, clunk.

Off to her right, a man sat on the edge of her bed. As he stood she saw that he was huge. A towering man who made her backpedal until she bumped into the wall.

He slapped the bloody bat into the palm of his hand.

Clunk, clunk, clunk.

Hannah shrank back and fell to the floor, frantically crawling until she collapsed onto her back. All the while, the man continued his slow approach toward her. He focused his deep, hateful eyes on her—eyes surrounded by a mask of blood spatter. The evil that was within this man radiated from him and paralyzed Hannah. She had seen some really bad things—unspeakable things—but this man was something different.

Evil.

Cold.

Hateful.

A killing machine.

She looked at him and he at her until he reached her. Then he simply stepped over her. She heard the front door open and close as he exited the home. Hannah lay there, her breath lost, her fear so heavy it pinned her still to the floor. But she had to get up and see what she already knew.

Using the walls to help her stand, her trembling legs had a hard time moving her forward. They were as heavy as cement pillars, and the floor may as well have been made of quicksand. Her limbs seemed to be reasoning with her, trying to hold her back to keep her from seeing the full picture.

"Trent?"

The stillness was interrupted only by the heavy pounding of her heart. The tremble was now *her*. If he did respond, she might not even be able to hear him over the volume of her own body.

When she finally made it to the bathroom, she looked at the blood beneath her feet. A red carpet walk to the worst horror show she'd ever seen. Trent's body was in the bathtub, wrapped in the nylon shower curtain. It looked like he'd been vacuum sealed. A piece of meat that needed to be thrown into the freezer before he spoiled.

'SS' with the devil's tail at the end of each letter was painted on the wall in what she assumed was Trent's blood. No cleaning agent would ever remove that stain. She couldn't get herself to move any closer or look any longer. What she had already seen could never be unseen.

Ever.

Like her father in that wheelchair.

And the dummy.

Backing out of the bathroom, she pulled the door closed and sat in the middle of the squeaky end of the bed. Where she and Trent always sat. Where the large man had stood from when he walked menacingly toward her. Everything moved so slowly. But it all had a tremble to it. Like a vibrating phone.

Her phone. It had somehow made it into her hand, and she managed to call Emily.

"I need you to come to my house," she said, sounding robotic. "They got Trent. There's so much blood."

She hung up, dropped the phone, and it bounced between her feet. She looked at the floor and at the bloody footprints that led her to this spot. She thought of the now faceless large man, Trent in the bathtub, and all the blood, and it made her cry so hard she quickly reached hysteria.

CHAPTER 18

respond

EMILY KNELT NEXT to Officer Maxwell. His eyes were closed, and his head rested on the door of the car. His breathing was slow and steady.

"I'm sorry, Dan," Emily said.

Maxwell opened one eye. "For what?"

Emily looked at the ground between her feet. Ed Powers, the dead officer covered next to Maxwell, was a haunting image she tried to ignore. If she treated it like a prop . . .

"For what happened to you." She nodded around. "For this."

"This isn't your fault. So you keep your apology and focus yourself on getting the bad guys." Maxwell grimaced. "You keep it because you're a good cop, and these animals are a bunch of thugs."

"I can't help but—"

"No," Maxwell said. "You can help it. Do police work, and nail these bastards. All of them. They've killed one of ours again, and that can't go unanswered. We don't let them get away with that. We don't let them do what they did all those years ago all over again. We don't."

"Yeah," Emily said and nodded. "This has changed me, Dan. I feel anger. I feel something dangerous building up inside of me. I'd held it in since I was a kid, and this, what they're doing, is bringing it out."

"I'm angry, too."

"I feel I should be the one to go and tell Ed's wife."

"You don't get to make that decision." He reached for her hand and gave it a squeeze, drawing her attention. "Protect yourself. Watch after your sister and mother."

He left a handprint of blood behind.

"I will," Emily said, everything around her so sad and crimson. "This is all happening so fast. I don't feel like I'm in control. I don't feel we can keep this powder keg we're sitting on from exploding."

"Yeah," Maxwell said and closed his eye and rested his head. The ambulance pulled up. "Whenever shit like this goes down time slows to a crawl, but afterward everything returns to normal, and perspective slams you in the face. Think before you do. Don't become reactive. That'll make you careless."

Emily stood. "OK, Dan." Her cell phone rang.

"You can stop this," he said. "Do what you must and remember who you're dealing with."

Emily turned away, withdrew the phone from her pocket, and looked at the screen. She immediately answered the call. "Hannah?" she said.

Emily listened to her sister's monotone voice. If the wind blew it would've knocked her over.

"You OK?" she managed to say.

Emily looked at the phone, put her ear to it again, and heard a thump.

"Officer? Are you hurt?" It was one of the paramedics.

"I don't know," Emily said. "Everything is happening all at once. I mean, no, I'm fine. It's just that everything is falling apart. These people are everywhere at once, dismantling us. They're like ants pouring out of a nest."

The man turned away, and Emily spotted Frerk. "Henry?"

He looked, and she motioned him over.

"We have to roll. They got to my sister."

"What?"

"My sister. They got to her."

"Ah, shit!"

Frerk hurried into the cruiser, and before Emily had closed her door, the tires squealed as the vehicle spun to gain traction on the cement. The wheels found purchase, and the cruiser took off, lights swirling and sirens wailing, a cloud of blue smoke behind them.

"What do you mean they got to your sister? Is she OK?"

Emily shook her head. "No, she's not. At least I don't think she is. She didn't say much and sounded bad. I think she's in shock." She lifted the phone and dialed the captain.

He picked up on the first ring. "Captain Patrick Creighton."

"Captain?"

"Emily?" A long pause. "You OK? You sound like shit. What's it like there?"

"A war zone, Captain. A goddamn war zone. I just got a call from my sister. They were there again. I—I think maybe they got to her or got her boyfriend."

"Jesus."

"They're spreading us thin, Captain. Picking us apart."

"I've dispatched two units to your mother's. They should be there soon. I'll update you once they take her into protective custody."

"She may not want to go."

"They're not leaving without her. That's the orders."

"Thank you, Captain. Make sure they know she needs to take her medicine with her."

"We'll take care of her. Your sister?"

"I'm going with Frerk now; we're en route. In case this is a homicide, we might want to be ready to roll crime scene."

"Be careful that you're not walking into a trap. Better yet, maybe you should come in. Sit this one out, and let your colleagues handle it. Who knows what you might see there."

"I can't, Captain. This is my sister, and I have to be there for her. I don't care what I see. I'm sure you understand."

"I do. You sound tired though, and I'm concerned."

"I'm concerned, too, Captain. Let me go and get my sister. She's going to need me. I have Frerk with me."

"I know, Em, you told me. Now focus, OK? Bring her in with you. She'll be safe here."

"I will, Captain. Thank you."

Emily hung up the phone. She hadn't realized how fast the vehicle was moving. Trees and houses and street signs whizzed past her; Frerk's knuckles were white from gripping the steering wheel.

"They're doing it again," Emily said. "They're doing it again, and I don't know how to stop them."

"One at a time," Frerk said, his awareness clearly on high alert. "We get them one at a time. Alive or dead makes no difference to me. But we get them before they get any more of us."

Emily sank into the seat of the speeding cruiser. "I prefer dead. We'd all be better off. Every single one of them dead this time. No loose ends."

CHAPTER 19

gone, just like that

THE YELLOW CRIME scene tape created an unspoken barrier that the media and gathered civilians didn't dare cross. Police and forensics were on location, securing and preserving the crime scene through photographic evidence; yellow numbered card tents counted the fallen bullet casings, which added up well into triple digits, and one even marked the body of Officer Powers. A white drape surrounded the fallen officer and kept him from the irreverent clicks of cell phone cameras and the zoom of lenses of local media that had begun to gather and broadcast live to professional news outlets and social media alike.

Everyone present could feel the hysteria of history repeating itself. The live news feeds would take care of most everyone watching, putting the public into full panic-mode.

Seasoned Officers Chris Forti and Karol Jones had taken Urban and Gwendolyn into custody. The officers had covered the heads of the juveniles with t-shirts to keep their faces hidden from onlookers.

"My father is going to get you all," Urban said.

The young man was so angry and filled with hate that it was palpable. Everyone they walked past on their way to the squad car had stopped and looked at him, their eyes wide, shock equal to the devastation around them. This was a taste of what they were dealing with.

"What are you so angry at?" Forti said.

"You and everyone like you ruin people's lives," Urban spat. "Shit isn't just brown, it's blue, too. You think you're doing good, but you're not. You interfere in people's lives. But this time, you've awakened a sleeping giant. People are looking, curious to know, and the Sinners will show them. There is something coming for you and everyone like you and maybe everyone watching!"

"I didn't do anything," Gwendolyn said from beneath the shroud that covered her face, her voice shrill as she struggled against Officer Jones' hold.

"We'll figure that out, but right now you're being detained and taken in for questioning," Jones said.

"For what?"

"We'll let you know when we get you there. Until then, I think it best you don't say anything at all because anything you say can and will be used against you."

"Oh, like I give a shit!" came her muffled reply.

"She didn't do anything," Urban shouted.

Forti kept his hand cupped around Urban's elbow and remained silent. He opened the back door to his squad car and placed a hand on top of Urban's head.

"Watch your head," Forti said and helped Urban into the car. He closed the door, muting the young man's venomous words with the confined space.

Jones put Gwendolyn into her squad car, purposely keeping the teenagers apart. Then both officers got inside their cruisers and drove the kids away from shouted questions and clicking cameras.

JOYCE FINISHED LOADING the children into a small bus.

"Are you sure you need to do this?" the officer asked.

"Yes, I'm sure."

"We can keep a detail on you. Nothing is going to happen."

Joyce slid into the driver's seat and spoke through the window she had rolled down.

"With all due respect, Officer . . .?" Her brows raised with the question.

"Bobby McDonald, ma'am."

"Well, Officer McDonald, after what I saw today, how violent these people are, I couldn't in good conscience have my children remain here.

The peace that surrounds the sanctuary I've built has been shattered. What sort of caregiver would I be if I were to stay? I have nothing to prove, and this isn't my fight—or theirs."

"I understand," Officer McDonald said. "We can't force you to stay."

"No," Joyce said and started the bus. "I've given my statement, and I've told the female officer that interviewed me exactly where I was going. What was her name?"

"Officer Meredith Finley."

"Yes, Officer Finley," Joyce nodded. "She was nice enough, and like you, she tried to convince me to stay, to not—" Joyce paused in thought—"'displace' my children. I think those were her words."

"I'm trying not to be pushy, but I agree with her," McDonald said. "Meredith knows we are capable of keeping you and the children safe. What the Sinners were after has been removed."

"I am concerned about retaliation. Look at all these children in the bus. I'm responsible for their well-being," Joyce said. "I have a lot of children to protect, and this decision—no matter the opinion of you, Officer McDonald, or that of Officer Finley—will sway me from not wanting to expose the children to more of what they've just been through. I won't keep them here—not another single moment."

Officer McDonald sighed, rested his hand on the butt of his gun, and surveyed the devastation, clearly resigned to the notion that Joyce was making the right decision after all.

"Is there anything I can do for you?"

"Yes," Joyce said and leaned out the window. She lowered her voice to a whisper. "You can catch these thugs. All of them. And put them away for a long time. I want to make sure when I come back with the children that they are safe."

Joyce put the vehicle in drive, and before she pressed on the gas, she said, "My kids will have counseling. I know how I felt and feel about what I saw. I can only imagine their terror."

"Good luck," Officer McDonald said, patted the side of the bus, and took a step back.

Joyce pulled away, and the police made a path so she could navigate through the crowd. Once she broke free of the gathering, she sped up and watched everyone fading in the rearview mirror with a sense of relief.

CHAPTER 20

aunt stefanie

BETO ENTERED STEFANIE'S house through the front door. No forced entry, just a twist of the knob and an open door as if it had been left that way on purpose.

"I've been expecting you," Stefanie said. She showed no fear. Beto raised the gun he held and aimed it between Stefanie's eyes.

"Who is in the house with you?"

Stefanie smiled. "No one. That is, until you decided to let yourself in."

Beto crept around, searching.

"I told you, no one else is here."

"Then you won't mind if I have myself a quick look."

"Suit yourself."

The place was small, and Beto easily performed a quick sweep. As Stefanie had said, it was indeed just the two of them.

"My fight with you and your stupid gang has been long over, don't you think?"

"Is that what you think, really?"

Stefanie nodded. "It is."

"So, you haven't thought about that day? It hasn't bothered you any that you were incapable of putting me down after all I had done?"

He stared at Stefanie but didn't get the reaction he sought. In fact, her smile remained and even widened some.

"You can't tell me that empty gun doesn't haunt you, that you can't still feel its useless weight in your grasp after I gunned down your friends?"

"I've tried to keep it from my mind and concentrate on raising the girls in an environment as normal as possible. My emotions needed to be disposable. That was how I coped. That was how I focused."

"Would it surprise you to know it bothered me that I just walked away from you? I should've finished things right there."

"No, I'm not surprised," Stefanie said. "We are two very different types of people. You don't seem to be the forgiving type. You cling onto everything negative and invite no good into your life. You create terror and hoard negativity."

"Don't fool yourself. I invite plenty of good into my life. It was there, this good, but then one day it was gone. That's happened to me twice now. And it's not that I don't forgive. It's more like I left a loose end. Allowed a way for the story to continue. And here we are, so many years later, at the next chapter."

"I suppose I did the same. Maybe we've finally come to the ending of the book? Skipped right to the final chapter. For the record, the difference between me and you is I've focused my energy on raising the girls, elevating them to something better than the slop you and your friends tried to roll them around in, leaving them orphaned and traumatized."

Beto laughed. "I worked on raising my son too, but I suppose my efforts are worth so much less than yours?"

"And you got a job? Stayed out of trouble? Made an honest living?"

"I provide."

"You evoke fear and mayhem. I'm done with you, Beto. My fight is now within my own body," Stefanie said.

"You have cancer, don't you?"

She nodded.

"I'm sorry."

"Me too. But forgive me if I tell you I have my doubts. You're sorry? Are you really?" Her sudden downtrodden expression was full of self-pity and internal struggle.

"I am. I didn't want things to be like this."

"Like this?"

"You, weakened."

"Sorry to disappoint."

"Unfortunately, our fight is not over. No matter how many times you say it, it won't change that fact until it reaches a climax—and *then* things will be finished. You see, your daughter . . ." Beto thought for a moment. "Your daughter—that's what you call her, isn't it?"

"Yes, they're my daughters. I've raised them as my own."

"How admirable. One of them had a part in taking my son and sticking him into the foster system. This has complicated my situation some."

"If she did it, then I'm sure there was a good reason. They know very little about what happened. I've made it my business to keep them far from that. They started calling me Mom not too long after our cultures collided and they'd realized both of their parents were gone. They needed to heal, and so did I. They gave me purpose. You were and have been the furthest thing from our minds. We're all so much better without you."

"The Sinners aren't responsible for their mother's suicide. She was weak. Unfit. A victim of her own pathetic existence. I won't lie and tell you I was sad about the lady offing herself because of her guilt. In fact, I found it amusing."

"You're a son of a bitch, Beto."

"Ahh, there's your spark. It's the same one I saw so long ago. You speak about such differences between the two of us, but yet you become so savage when you need to be. A little hypocritical, don't you think?"

"Heartbreak and digging into memories better left buried can do that, yes. It can bring out anger, drive someone to desperation. Make them think foolish thoughts and act on rash decisions."

"So you understand my position then?"

Stefanie looked at Beto and then out the window. "I do."

"The only way you get returned in one piece is if they return my son. But knowing you're sick, I'll give you a chance to get your meds, and I'll be gentle. Unless you force me to do otherwise."

"Regardless of what you think, our fight is indeed over. What I say doesn't require a rebuttal." Stefanie stood. Her movement was slow, and she grimaced as she limped with each step. "Am I supposed to show you gratitude for this?"

Beto laughed. "No. You're merely collateral to help me get my son back. I don't care about you in the least."

"I'm infected with the big C. I only wish it were contagious."

"Vicious. So, so vicious."

"My usefulness has run dry."

"Don't underestimate your importance to your children. You'll be useful—trust me. Your daughters love you too much."

"Trusting you and your lackeys is something I could never do. Who knows, maybe I'm the one that has use for you."

Beto laughed. "Sure. I could only imagine what that could be."

Stefanie smiled at him and then worked on gathering her medicines. "You amuse me, Beto."

CHAPTER 21

taken

OFFICERS GARRETT MCLELLAN and Tom Kelly jumped out of the squad car and sprinted to Stefanie's front door. Officer McLellan knocked on the door with the handle of his flashlight while officer Kelly hurried to the windows. He cupped his hands around his eyes to get a look inside the house.

"Stefanie, this is Officer McLellan. We need you to open the door, please."

He pounded harder on the door, waited a moment, then radioed dispatch. "There's no response at the residence."

"Breach," dispatch responded.

Officer McLellan pulled his weapon out of the holster and lifted his foot, planting it forcefully next to the doorknob. Wood splintered, and the door slammed open. He entered the house, swinging his gun to the left and right as his eyes followed the tip of the weapon. His partner joined him, and together they swept room to room. Officer Kelly kept a hand on his partner's shoulder and was responsible for watching their flank.

"Clear," McLellan said and lowered his weapon.

"Damn it," Kelly said. He depressed the button on his radio. "House is clear. No sign of struggle."

McLellan holstered his weapon. "I've got a bad feeling about this."

"Yeah, me too. We're at war with people that won't hesitate to kill anyone in their way and now they have Emily's mother. The worst-case scenario just got worse."

CHAPTER 22

receiving news

EMILY AND HANNAH sat on the stoop. They were close to one another, silence between them. The bustle of many officers going in and out of the apartment, tagging Trent's crime scene, had become background noise to both of them.

Hannah had a blanket wrapped around her shoulders. Her face was red, her eyes wet, and a certain tremble accompanied her existence.

"This was all coordinated, wasn't it?" Hannah said.

"Yes, they're showing tremendous organization."

"Aunt Stefanie?" She shook her head. "Mom?"

Emily rested her elbows on her knees and let her eyes drift to the cement between her feet. The speckles were like stars in the sky, but these were falling stars.

"I asked Captain Creighton to send a unit over there. They should be there by now. They're taking her into protective custody. She's safe."

"Can you check?" Hannah whimpered. "I can't help but think one thing is a distraction to do something else, and Mom was in their sights all along. That would give them leverage. That would hurt us worse than a dummy in a wheelchair, and especially what they did to Trent."

"They didn't get to her," Emily said. "And Trent——"

"Please, just check," Hannah said.

"OK. I'll radio in to make sure."

"Thank you."

Emily engaged her radio. "224 moving to an 85."

Emily turned a dial on her radio.

"Captain?"

"I'm here, Emily."

"My mother?"

There was silence.

"Captain?"

"I'm still here." Emily heard a loud sigh over the radio. "They got to your mother before we did."

A warm sensation moved through Emily's body. Dread pressed down on top of her, and her mind rejected what she had heard. "They what?"

"What did he just say to you?" Hannah asked and stood, the blanket falling. Her focus locked on her sister, and an explosion couldn't have stolen it away. "Emily?" she said. Her need to know widened her eyes, and her heart pounded fiercely. Her tone revealed that she suspected the worst.

"Can you repeat, Captain?"

"Is your sister with you?"

"Yes."

"Stay close to each other. It is as you said. They're pulling us apart by separating us. We'll get your mother back. We know he's going to try and use her as leverage to exchange her for his son. That's his only play."

"Yeah, his only play," Emily repeated. Her thoughts trailed off. "Captain, this is bad."

"It'll be OK. Whatever he wants is already a done deal. We'll give him the kid and whatever else he wants. We will get your mother back. I'm not going to let anything happen to her."

Emily pressed the button and then let it go. Words were hard to come by. She took out her earpiece and opened the radio communication so that Hannah could hear.

"When we do the exchange," the Captain said, "we're going to walk away. Priority one is getting your mother as far away from them as we can. Her safety is paramount. When they think they've gotten away, we will get them. I'll have them followed by plain clothes. Tell your sister I'm sorry for her loss. What happened to her boyfriend is a tragedy."

Emily moved the radio closer. "She can hear you, Captain. You're on speaker."

"Hannah, we will get them for what they did. To the both of you. And your mother, too."

Emily moved like she was made of clay. "Thanks, Cap. We both appreciate you," she said and turned off her radio.

"Do you think they're going to hurt her?" Hannah asked as she retrieved the fallen blanket. Her eyes were big red glassy balls.

"No. I think the captain has it exactly right. Beto intends to use Mom as a way to get his son back. Maybe we do it exactly as the captain says. We give him what he wants."

"This doesn't feel real," Hannah said and cried into her hands. "All of this craziness, and for what? Because my coworker took a sick day, and I was assigned to complete that case for her?"

Emily couldn't cry if she wanted to. Anger had risen in her chest, and it remained there, awaiting release. This was how she coped. Whoever was around when she was able to give in to her anger and release it . . . it was almost a certainty it would be a murderous occasion.

"That chance encounter is like the one that turned Dad into a vegetable and started an all-out gang war here in Battleground."

"Don't call it that."

"What?"

"Battleground."

"OK. Bellmore."

"Thank you."

"It *has* happened again. What are the chances?" She paused and laughed. "Maybe there's no other way out of this than to start thinking like them."

"I thought you wanted to give them what they wanted for Mom's sake?"

Emily took her backup firearm out of the ankle holster and gave it to her sister. "The gun is loaded. The safety is on. You know how to use it. Don't you dare hesitate if it's needed."

Hannah nodded, took the weapon, and slid it under the blanket that wrapped her body.

"They tried to get their kid out of the foster care home by sending a car full of thugs toting high-powered assault rifles. Officers arrived at the same time, and they had a gunfight in the middle of the street."

"What?"

"Like cowboys and Indians going at it. We were outmatched with their weapons, but our officers managed to hold their position and force a retreat."

"My God."

"One officer is dead, and we're not sure how many, but at least one of the gang members involved in the shootout was hit. Blood stained the street. It looked like a war zone."

"Emily, these people—"

"Are scum. It is now about survival for us, Hannah. What they did to Trent . . . I'm sure that was meant for you. When it wasn't you, it became a message to you. To us. You said he looked at you, stepped over you, and left. That's a message."

Hannah's face was streaked with tears. "His eyes were so evil."

"I know what you saw was terrible, and it will never leave you. I know you've lost a lot today, but you've got to push the tears back and get strong. It may save your life."

"I can't just flip this invisible switch like you can."

"You're going to need to, Hannah."

Hannah fell silent, then said, "I'm pregnant, Emily."

Emily went numb. "Wait, what?"

"Me and Trent . . . we're twelve weeks along. I wanted to tell you and Mom. Make it a big surprise with the ultrasound pictures I have." She cried. "Had. They were on the dresser in the bedroom. The dresser was covered with Trent's blood."

Tears burned Emily's eyes. She reached out and rubbed her sister's belly, and tears streaked her cheeks too.

"More of a reason to push them tears down. Your child needs his mother to be strong."

Emily stood and kissed Hannah's cheek.

"I love you, sis. I can't believe I'm going to be an aunt. It seems there's a break in the gathering storm clouds after all. Mom is going to be so happy when she finds out. I can't wait to tell her she's going to be a grandma."

Hannah smiled but cried hard. So hard she couldn't talk; she could barely stand.

Emily walked away.

"Emily?" Hannah called out, her voice weak and broken up.

Emily got to her squad car, and before she got inside, she looked at Hannah. "I love you, sis. No matter what happens, know that I love you and I did the best I could to help you and Mom. And if for some reason I don't see you again, you make sure that baby knows who I am."

Hannah hurried forward. "Emily!

Emily slid into the seat, slammed the door, started the engine, and drove away. She embraced the rage that simmered within and had begun to surface. She pounded the steering wheel and shouted out. The veins in her neck bulged, and her face reddened.

"What did you do to us? What did you do?"

CHAPTER 23

station arrival

OFFICER FORTI OPENED the rear passenger door to his cruiser, unbuckled Urban, and said, "We're here. Let me get you inside."

"I'm not going anywhere with you, pig!" Urban said and tried to dig in.

Just then, Officer Jones pulled in with Gwendolyn in the back seat of her patrol car.

"I told you, she didn't do anything," Urban said.

"That's not for us to decide," Forti said. "Now come out of the car or I'll force you out."

"You're real tough when you have my hands cuffed behind my back. Why don't you see how you do if you uncuff me?"

Forti reached into the vehicle and grabbed Urban by the cusp of his arm. He gave a gentle tug. "Come on, man. I understand you're pissed, and I would be too. But let's not turn this into something more than it already is."

Urban dropped his head and went limp. "What the hell do you know?" He turned and kicked Forti and then spit at him, soiling his shirt. Forti pushed Urban's face into his lap, holding him in place until Officers Robert Pratt and Glen Notaro rushed out of the processing building and assisted in laying him flat. They zip-tied his legs and placed a net over his head.

The officers dragged Urban out of the vehicle and carried him into the precinct by the ankles and wrist restraints. They moved him into a windowless holding room, unbound his ankles, and cuffed him to a steel loop embedded into a stainless-steel tabletop.

The steel table and chair were mounted to the floor, immovable.

"My father is going to kill all you pigs," Urban shouted and pulled against his restraints. The chains clanked but easily held. "All of you! Your mothers, fathers, babies, and everyone you know!"

The officers closed the heavy door and locked it.

"Isn't he a pleasure," Forti said.

Pratt laughed. "Wish I had one just like'im."

"Just like his dad, from what I hear," Notaro said.

"The town is erupting again," Forti said. "It's living up to its nickname. The captain's on edge, and Emily's family is coming apart before her eyes like it did when she was a kid. At least that's what I was told about that gang war from way back when."

"She was a kid," Notaro said.

"Yes, she was," Pratt said. He had a full head of gray hair and a face lined from age and worry. A veteran of the force. He looked at his fellow officers with a deep concern in his eyes. "If these guys are anything like they were back then, they're one of the most violent gangs I have ever seen and fought against. Nothing is off limits. This town became a war zone, and both sides lost so many because of one senseless act of drinking and driving."

"What is their gig anyways? I mean, what are they after?" Notaro said.

"Turf control and a show of power. A message to other gangs and us. They have no fear of authority. The last standing member of the gang disappeared about fifteen years ago and seems to have suddenly resurfaced."

"Why?"

Pratt shrugged. "Maybe he went away long enough to allow things to simmer down. But now that he's back, we know they were getting ready to reestablish themselves again. That little smart ass we just chained down like the animal he was raised to be is the cub of the guy who disappeared."

"Oh man," Forti said.

"Oh man is right. The screwed-up part?" Pratt said and then sighed. "Way back when, two little twin girls were left with no parents and a dead uncle. Their lives were shattered. The uncle, a police officer, served out of this very station. He was killed in the line of duty, facing off with the gang that called themselves the Southside Sinners. Those young girls, well, of course you know Emily, but her sister? Her name is Hannah, and she's a social worker of some sort. Guess who so happened to remove that mouthy kid inside that other room from his home?"

A stunned silence inserted itself.

"What are the chances?" Forti said, the fragile calm shattered like glass.

"I would've thrown the F-word somewhere in there," Pratt said. "I'm telling you guys—this is going to get messy."

"It already is."

"C'mon, let's go help Karol get the other one out of her car. I'm sure she's just as bad as this one."

The group of officers moved together to assist their fellow officer. This was their show of force, and they did it in unity.

"And what are we supposed to do with them?"

"The captain doesn't want either one of them out of our custody."

"So, we're babysitting these kids?"

"It seems we are."

"Great. Who gets to change their diapers?"

The officers laughed and stepped out of the building where they found Officer Jones in a struggle with Gwendolyn. She was trying to get her out of the car.

"Get your hands off of me, you damn pig!"

CHAPTER 24

joy ride

"YOUR CAR RIDES nice," Beto said from behind the steering wheel.

"I'm so glad you like it," Stefanie said. "Insert sarcasm."

Beto laughed. "You didn't need to tell me you were being sarcastic."

"You know, when you're sick like I am, you tend not to care too much about things like this."

She felt Beto watch her as she stared out the passenger side window.

"A car." She tapped the window. "It's not the materialistic things like this. It's the beauty of nature. The blue of the sky, the white fluff of the clouds, and the tickle of a cool breeze on your skin. Of course, the warmth of the sun becomes something bigger when you have a ticking time bomb inside. Your loved ones and how much they mean to you."

"So you've become this deep thinker with some profound introspection now?" Beto grunted.

"It all seems so meaningless as you start to prepare to face the end. I suppose somewhere in there is hope that your life had some meaning that would be long-lasting. A mark. A significant impression. Something forever . . . but that's just fantasy." She chuckled. "I'm at the point now where all I care about are Hannah and Emily. It is my job as their mother to continue to protect them."

"You're their aunt, not their mother. Their real mother gave up on life. She killed herself. She's dead."

"I may not be their biological mother, but that doesn't take away the fact that I nurtured them, helped them outgrow people like you. I did my job. I made my mark and left a significant impact. You leave devastation. I want you to take my life. Finish what was left undone so long ago. Come out the winner."

Beto laughed. "I appreciate the offer, and as tempting as it sounds, I'm not sure it would be as satisfying as it once could've been. Besides, one of your daughters is responsible for taking my son away. I'm going to use you to get him back."

"And how do you propose to do that?"

"You're a bargaining piece, Stefanie, of course. They'd gladly exchange my son for you. You with all of your defects and disease still have a use." Beto laughed. "Why do you think they think so highly of you? Like you said—you've mothered them! Cared for them and brought them into adulthood. And you claim you did it without allowing what happened to them as a child to define them. Bravo. You did a crappy job."

Stefanie stared at the side of Beto's head. Her hands balled into tight fists. He had no right to talk about the relationship between her and her daughters like that. Despite what he said, she knew she did a good job. All he did was destroy relationships. How could the two even compare?

A well-placed fist to the side of his face would do him some good. But her hand loosened. She had no strength to do any real harm and would probably only hurt herself in the process. Maybe, just maybe, there would be a proper ending to this. For that, she would save her strength.

"Why was your son taken?" Stefanie said and settled into the seat.

"Retaliation because of what happened years ago. That's the only thing that makes sense to me." Beto watched the road; his head moved left and right and to the rearview mirror. "I mean what are the chances that your daughter—" he looked at Stefanie "—just happened to be the one to take my son away from his mother? I said it, *your daughter*. She's the one that actually removed him from the house. I wonder if she thought herself powerful? Scaring a child like that. Do you think she enjoyed what she did?"

Stefanie thought. "My daughters aren't looking to seek revenge for what happened twenty years ago. I've taught them better. They probably didn't even know who you were, other than a name, until yesterday."

"I doubt that."

"What do you know anyway? You have an illegitimate child with a woman that is unfit to care for her kid . . . your kid." Stefanie laughed. "Supposedly your child anyway. A woman like her, who knows? She can't do it properly and the state has to take him away, and that somehow becomes an act of purposeful aggression toward you?"

Beto nodded. "*Jugada estúpida.*"

"English, please."

"I said 'stupid play.' They should've thought things through."

"You know what you are, Beto?"

"Do tell."

"You're a shadow, and you only cast darkness. There is no light in you. Never has been."

"Now you're just being hurtful." He laughed.

"How old are you now?"

Beto looked at Stefanie, and now she was looking at him.

"In my mid-forties. Why?"

"So you were in your mid-twenties at the time we first crossed paths. I was in my forties. I knew better at that age." She stared at him. "Why don't you?"

"Cute." Beto laughed. "I know well enough that the bad blood between my family and yours hasn't found resolve. Fate's a bitch, isn't it?"

Stefanie didn't answer.

"But this time around, I know it will find resolve. This can't go on forever. This vicious cycle will come to an end. Twenty years is long enough."

"You think this is going to be resolved by more senseless violence and death?"

"If that's what it takes, then yes."

Beto's phone rang and he answered it.

"Hola."

He paused, listening.

"*Esperate, déjame ir a algún lugar más privado.*"

Beto pulled the vehicle to the side of the road, killed the engine, took the keys, and exited the car. He strode away, and Stefanie watched as his expression contorted and turned to anger.

"ARE YOU SURE?" Beto fired off in rapid Spanish.

"I'm sure," Mateo replied in kind. "They brought him and another girl into the precinct less than five minutes ago."

"How did he look?"

"Pissed off. He must've been fighting like crazy. They bound his arms and legs and had a spit net over his head."

"They what? They put a covering over my son's head like he's a rabid dog or something?"

"That's not all," Mateo said. "They carried him in by his ankles and wrists. Treated him like an animal, man."

"You have guns?" Beto said.

"We do."

"How many are with you?"

"Five others besides me."

"Who?"

"Diego, Alejandro, Felipe, Rodrigo, and Alonso."

"You feeling up to going in, kicking things up a notch?"

Beto heard Mateo move his mouth away from the phone's mouthpiece, and pressed his ear firmly against his phone to listen.

"You guys feel like going in? Masks?"

A chorus of voices came buzzing through the phone. "They're ready. Masks on, guns firing?"

"Sinners sinning," Beto said.

"If we can't get out, we'll take as many of them with us as we can. Send a message."

"Ah, Mateo . . . tell the boys—"

"They know. Get your son back if we cannot."

Beto hung up the phone, slid it into his pocket, and returned to the car. His mind was troubled, knowing that he might be sending his men to a potential slaughter. These were his best men, and he couldn't afford to lose control. They needed to use surprise to their advantage.

CHAPTER 25

standoff

EMILY PARKED HER car one street over from Vicki's residence. Having been to this decaying, neglected neighborhood enough times to know how the locals dressed, she'd arrived in ratty sweatpants and a hoodie. She felt like she fit right in. Emily gripped a Taser hidden in her jacket pocket. It was charged and ready to go. Certain she could find a good use for it, she'd collapsed her expandable baton and tucked it into her waistband.

Deep inside the hood she seethed in anger, driven by her lust for revenge for all the things that had happened over the past two days—and for everything that happened when she was a child. Too much time had been stolen from her and her sister by people like Vicki and Beto.

These people and their way of life . . . she grimaced. They were ignorant, their education coming from the streets, and they only understood violence. Her father didn't have the chance to know that, but her uncle did. They brought him and so many from the police force down to their level. Uncle Glenn met them with violence and crippled them for years. It was the only thing they responded to. It was the only way. That was a lesson to her, and she would do the same, but this time, she'd finish them all for good. The scream in her head continued, and she clenched her fists at the madness.

Emily knocked on Vicki's door, and after a few moments, Vicki cracked the door open. "Marie?"

"Not quite," Emily said and drove her shoulder into the door, which sent Vicki stumbling backward. The woman's heavy, unfit body pounded the floor as she fell in a heap.

Storming into the house, Emily slammed the door and pulled out the Taser. She hit Vicki in the neck with the electric arc, and her body convulsed as she squealed and even pissed herself.

Emily whipped out the baton, and it clicked open. A forceful blow to the head and repeated strikes to the body gave the much larger woman no chance to fight back. Blood trickled from the splits in her scalp and nose. She was splayed now, lips fattened and teeth coated with blood. She slipped in the puddle of her own urine as she struggled to gain her bearings.

"Your boyfriend sent a man to kill my sister," Emily growled. "They got her boyfriend instead. They beat him to death with a bat. That's what I've come here to do to you. Ojo por ojo."

With all her might, Emily kicked Vicki in the ribs. Vicki shouted out and gasped for air and held her side.

"That is for treating your son like crap and starting this shit," Emily said, landing a blow with each word she spoke. "This. Is. Your. Fault!"

"You can't do this," Vicki groaned as blood spilled from her mouth. "You're a cop."

"No, not anymore. I left that behind hours ago when I found out what happened at my sister's house."

"What? You . . . you're going to punish me for trying to do the same thing for my son? I was trying to protect him!"

"No, you were starting World War Three! You've succeeded in turning Bellmore back into Battleground!"

"Motherly instinct—"

"You don't have any of that, so don't even try and act like you've given your son the love he needs to grow. I knew what you were doing when you called him! You knew what Beto was going to do in retaliation!"

"That's his son too! He has the right to know!"

Emily used the wall for leverage and balance as she unloaded another barrage of kicks, finishing with heavy, brutal stomps. "Now he took my mother! My fucking mother! He thinks he's going to take another mother away from me? I'll take everything from him! I'll start right here with you! No one will care. No one will miss you! You are no better than the filth you're lying in. Then I'll move onto that loser son of yours! Stomp you all out like the cockroaches you are!"

Vicki curled into a ball and tried to cover her vulnerable areas. Emily switched to using the baton, covered in red, but soon backed away, exhausted.

"Now tell me where your asshole boyfriend is before I follow through with what I'm thinking about doing to you."

Vicki rolled her head, her body coated with sweat, dirt, and blood. "I don't know."

"You know," Emily said through clenched teeth as she struck Vicki over and over. Again, with each blow she spoke. "I. Asked. You. Where. Is. Your. Boyfriend!"

Vicki's arms were bruised and bleeding from the lashing she failed to fend off. Lumps had already begun to form all over her body from the brutal beating she'd endured.

"OK. OK."

Emily stopped, tired and out of breath.

"He's on his way to your house."

"My house?"

"Element of surprise, I suppose." She coughed and drooled blood. "I don't know his reasoning. I'm his old lady. You know how that works?"

"Yeah," Emily said and collapsed the baton. "You should be used to the beatings then. You and your thug friends have started something that can end only one way. All of this because you can't keep your nose clean and straighten out your life. You are to blame for this. You! If you didn't make that phone call, had just followed the advice of the counselor and actually attempted to improve things around here, this never would've happened. If not for you, you should've done it for your son. All of this could've been avoided."

"I didn't want to keep the baby and bring him up in this environment, but Beto did. If I would've gone against his wishes, he would've killed me."

"That would've been so terrible for everyone. I feel so sorry for you."

"Screw off."

"Make sure you tell him I did this. Show him your wounds. That is, if you get to see him before I do. I'm going to kill him when I see him. He won't get the same chance you had. I'm not walking away from him until he's dead. Your son is going to have no father because of your stupid decisions. Give me your phone."

Vicki handed it to her and Emily smashed the screen with heavy stomps. "In case you were thinking about warning him I was coming."

Emily turned to walk out of the filthy house. "Oh, one more thing," she said, her lungs burning. "If anything happens to my mother or my sister, I will kill every single one of you. I will have nothing to lose. And what I do to you will make this look like it was just a spanking."

CHAPTER 26

head-on collision

SERGEANT LISA TEST sorted reports from behind the large, semi-circular wooden platform desk. Beyond the desk was the empty waiting room. Things had gone quiet in the precinct since the Sinners had started shooting up the streets like they were in the Wild West. "Did you get him into the room?" she asked without moving her eyes from her task.

"Yeah, he's in," Officer Pratt said.

"Pleasant kid?"

Pratt laughed. "One of the sweetest in all my years of law enforcement. Could use a good behind swatting, if you ask me."

"So I've heard," Test said. "Thanks for giving me something to smile about. Not much to laugh about right now."

"No, there's not," Pratt said, and his voice fell off. Something about this silence felt worse than a shootout with a ruthless gang. The quiet carried the sorrow of the bloodbath that took place only hours ago. "It almost feels wrong knowing—"

"Captain Creighton is working hard on putting a task force together so we can take these guys down," Test said.

"Good. Getting a little payback for Powers and Bebout will do everyone some good."

"Don't call her that. She hates it."

"Yeah, it's Emily, I know. I made that mistake once."

"The captain wants all hands on deck," Balzafiore said as she entered the room.

Test looked at her. "How are you doing?"

110

"Putting it aside so I can remain useful. Every single one of us are needed," she said with shoulders held up high. "Even Maxwell got patched up and is staying. There's a briefing coming within the hour. Don't know if you heard, but they got Bebout's mother."

"Are you freaking kidding me?"

"I hate to say it, but fate has it out for those sisters," Pratt said. "They can't catch a break. They've got balls, these Sinners. Big ones."

"Balls? Yes. Stupid? Quite," Test said. "They're going to find out Emily isn't one to stand by and watch things collapse all around her. I think she's been carrying around this anger since she was a kid, and it's going to come exploding out."

A Hispanic male approached the desk. A clear 'SS' tattoo could be seen on his neck. Both Officers Pratt and Test dropped their hands to their sidearms and gave the handles a firm grip.

"*Estoy aquí para ver a Urban.*"

"Do you speak English?" Test said, her senses on high alert.

"I do," Mateo said. "*Nos vamos a matar a ustedes.*"

"I said English," Test said, her patience short, her trust unwilling to keep her from lifting her sidearm out of its holster.

"I said I'm here to see Urban," Mateo said.

"He's in our custody right now and is not allowed visitors."

"Is he under arrest?"

"He's been detained and is under custody of the state."

Mateo slammed his fist on top of the desk, and in response, Pratt lifted his sidearm out of its holster and pointed it at the man.

"*Muertos,*" Mateo said, pointing at each of them with his fingers in the shape of a gun. "*Todos.*"

Pratt walked to the front of the desk and grabbed Mateo's arm while Test radioed, "Twenty-five at the front desk."

Mateo shrugged off the hold and dashed toward the exit. Pratt started after him. "Hey, stop where you are!"

"Let him go," Test said. Then, calling after the man, "If you come back in here, we're going to arrest you!"

Mateo turned around and saw a group of about eight officers pouring into the waiting room from the back. "Yeah, sure." He laughed, turned, and exited.

"You see how brazen these bastards are?" Test said.

"I think they're testing our bravery," Balzafiore said.

"That's real smart," McDonald said. "Coming in here after one of his thug friends gunned down one of our own." He looked at Test. "Are you sure we should've let him go?"

"This may be our chance to start pulling them off the streets," Officer Mike Edwards said.

"We don't do anything until Captain Creighton briefs us," Test said.

The group eased up, and Officers Test and Pratt rested their guns back into their holsters.

"Who is coming for the kid, and when are they supposed to arrive?" Forti asked.

"Social Services. But not until things calm down and we can ensure the safety of the social worker."

Most of the officers broke away from the conversation and returned to the back, immersing themselves in their work again.

Just then, six armed men with masks, bulletproof vests, and automatic weapons entered the lobby. Before Test could react, the men opened fire and sprayed her with bullets, rapidly tearing her face and chest apart, dropping her where she stood. The discharged weapons barely made a sound thanks to silencers.

"Don't grab for your gun," the muffled voice of an attacker said, quickly locking Officer Edwards into a choke hold. With an arm around his neck, the masked assailant used the cop's body as a shield. The intruders followed in a tight group, moving in through the door beside the desk and entering a large open area with many desks piled with paperwork and ringing phones. The officers on desk duty moved here and there, oblivious.

"Sinners Sinning!" Alejandro shouted, and all the officers turned. They drew their weapons and ran for cover.

Mateo put the gun to the side of Edwards' head and pulled the trigger. The silent weapon sprayed brain matter and tissue across the room, and Edwards went limp, held up by the masked man.

The Sinners opened fire, focusing on Officers McDonald, Forti, and Jones, who tried to use their desks as cover. They didn't stand a chance. The hail of oncoming bullets prevented any chance they had at returning fire. They fell to the spray of gunfire that ripped through the furniture and their bodies.

Officers Press, Maxwell, and Frerk fired at the same time, dropping Diego, Alonso, and Felipe. The three remaining gunmen—Alejandro, Rodrigo, and Mateo—turned their weapons on those officers instead.

Papers flew and trinkets on the desks exploded; the sound was deafening, and blue smoke filled the air. Panicked voices overtaken by adrenaline and fear had the officers shouting instructions to one another.

Officers Balzafiore, Finley, Mclellan, and Kelly emerged from another room. They were off to the side of the gunmen and opened fire, each dropping men and unloading their firearms until they'd emptied their magazines.

Then everything went quiet.

Frerk stood up from the other side of the room. Maxwell and Press did not.

Pratt entered the room and stood frozen, assessing what had transpired. Shock covered Frerk's face.

Balzafiore, Finley, Mclellan, and Kelly spread out and checked their fallen friends. Six gunmen dead; seven officers dead. Blood everywhere.

The devastation within the precinct was like nothing they had ever seen.

"The kid," Balzafiore shouted, hurried through a different side door, and entered the room Urban had been placed in. The kid remained shackled to the table. He looked at the officer and smiled while giving her the finger.

"I hope all your friends are dead."

"You little bastard!"

"You people don't listen. I told you. They'll do anything to get me back. Anything!"

Balzafiore smacked the kid and repeatedly punched him. She didn't stop until Pratt pulled her away.

"Beating him isn't going to stop them. Get ahold of yourself."

"Get ahold of myself!" she panted. "Get ahold of myself? Are you kidding me right now?"

"No, I'm not kidding you. You have to keep control over your emotions. If you don't, you are no better than them."

"You hit me! You hit me!" Urban shouted, and his mouth bled.

"They just invaded the precinct and killed our friends, turned it into a bloodbath."

"I know what they did," Pratt said and pulled Balzafiore close, hugging her until she cried—and so did he.

"Oh, boo-hoo," Urban said and laughed. "Child beater, boo-hoo. They'll be coming back for you."

CHAPTER 27

pain

EMILY ENTERED HER house, her 9mm leading the way.

"We're in here," Beto said. "*Tenemos que llegar a un acuerdo.*"

"Yes," Emily said. "We do need to make a deal."

She stopped and pressed her back against the wall opposite the kitchen. "Mom?"

"I'm here, baby."

"How are you?"

"Fine."

"Did he bring anyone else with him?"

"No. Not that I know of."

"I didn't bring anyone," Beto said. "This here is between you, me, and your mother. I wish your sister were here so, whatever the outcome, she could see it completed. This can all end right here, right now. Give us closure."

"How so?" Emily said, and her hands squeezed the handle of the gun; her finger hugged the trigger, ready. Unsure what she would see when she turned the corner and stepped into the kitchen, the thought of ending it her way was the first thing on her mind. She was in control. He was just a thing in her way. A removable and vulnerable thing.

If she had a clear shot, she was going to take it. The likelihood that he wasn't using her mother as a shield was slim, but there was a chance.

"We talk. We sort this out without violence."

Emily laughed. "An officer was left dead in the streets. Shot at the foster home your son was taken to. And you somehow think we've moved to negotiations?"

"Either that or we start shooting right now."

"Tempting."

"You know how it goes, Officer. These things happen. Casualties of war."

"So this is war?"

"Declared the moment they took my son and held him captive."

"I'm coming in."

"Please do, but be smart and do it slowly. Yes? Watch where you point that gun, too. It seems all three of us here are nervous and have little to lose if someone reacts too quickly, wouldn't you say?"

Emily raised her weapon and slowly crept around the corner. Beto had her mother in front of him, an arm draped over her shoulder and wrapped around her body, his head half hidden behind hers. He peered out from behind her. *Like a coward*, Emily thought. His other hand held a gun, and he pointed it steadily at Emily and then returned it to Stefanie's head.

"So, what are we going to do here?" Emily asked as her finger wrapped the trigger a little tighter; a snake coiling its victim before it used all of its strength to squeeze the life out of the prey.

"We're going to discuss how this trade will work. So yes, we're down to talk now."

"Do you think Captain Creighton is going to allow me to just hand your son over when the state put him into protective custody?"

"Well, that sounds like a problem that you're going to have to work on. You get your mother back when I get my son. No harm will come to her. She will continue to take her medicine, and she will continue to wither until the disease she has kills her. Until then, she will be well taken care of. The exchange is going to be simple. Her for him. That's the only way this works."

Emily relaxed. The deal would be impossible to make. Beto already implied that more people were going to die, and that meant the Sinners were up to something. Whatever the case, she was betting on the gang falling one at a time. And here she was, hoping for Beto to be the first.

"OK," she said. "How do you suppose we do this?"

"My son gets dropped off at a destination of my choosing. He is taken into custody by one of my people, and when I know he is secure, I will tell you where your aunt is."

Emily stared at Beto. The deep, pitted anger she felt toward him had to remain with her for now, pressed down into a place where it would be easily accessible once it could be unleashed. Anger, when used at the proper time and for the right reasons, could help to keep herself and others alive.

"How do I know you're going to tell me where she is once you get your son? That you're not going to hurt her?"

Beto shrugged. "You don't. There are no guarantees, but I can see no other way for me to trust the police. Especially when it seems you have the upper hand against me. Besides, your mother is sick enough that I don't need to do anything more than what time and her disease are doing for me. I want my son back. And when I have what I want, you can have her. Enjoy what little time you have left to complete your task. But you'll need to hurry."

"So, you're a man of your word all of a sudden?" Emily stared and waited for a response. "Someone to be trusted?"

Beto remained still, his unanswered offer hanging in the air.

"Excuse me, if you will," Emily said. "But I have a hard time believing anything you say. I mean, given our history, you could understand why, couldn't you?"

"I can appreciate that," Beto said. "I have a hard time trusting you too. Your sister. She's the one that took our son from the house. It should be her standing in front of me, not you or your aunt."

"She was acting on someone else's behalf."

"It doesn't matter." Beto laughed and waved the gun. "Don't you see? We're connected. A universal paradox. Maybe we're meant to play this cat and mouse game forever. I suppose in some ways I do have the upper hand because I don't have to play by the rules of the law like you do."

"I think you misunderstand me. I am not here as a police officer. I'm here as someone that's protecting my family from a criminal and his fragile empire. A coward has-been that ran away after a fight to lick his wounds, and now he thinks he can come back and intimidate me and my family."

"You're just like your uncle, I see."

"The value I place on the lives of my mother and sister far exceed my own."

"A martyr then? How noble."

"Not really. A loving daughter and sister. Someone that upholds family values, makes an honest living, and tries to help serve those in need. Protect them against people like you and your friends."

"Nice speech," Beto said. "If I had two free hands I might even applaud you. Now let's talk about the exchange."

"Shut up, Beto," Stefanie said.

"Now, now," he said and tightened his hold. "I thought you said our quarrel was over."

"The more I stand here and listen to you, your arrogance, and the way you talk to my daughter, the more I wish there was a bullet in that gun that day I put it to the back of your head!"

Beto laughed and tapped the barrel of his gun on Stefanie's head. "But there's bullets in mine now."

"I hope you're ready to prove it," Stefanie said and quickly turned around.

Beto fumbled, losing his grip as he staggered backward in his surprise. Stefanie wiggled free of his hold.

"Mom, no!" Emily shouted and lunged forward.

Stefanie reached for the gun, and Beto pulled it away. Stefanie kept moving forward and clawed his face and growled wildly.

Blam!

Beto fell to the floor and froze, clearly in shock. "What just happened?" Blood trickled from the deep scratches. He held his ears in the ringing aftermath of the gunshot. He stared at Emily, who was frozen, disconnected from the now, staring at her mother.

"Mom!" Emily said and tried to assess the situation. Everything was red and thick. Unrealistic and far away.

"Why would you do that?" Beto said to Stefanie.

Time stopped as Emily took in the scene before her: Her mother held her stomach, and blood poured out of the hole in her gut. Stefanie turned, faced Emily, and fell to her knees, her mouth a perfect circle, her eyes glossy and filled with pain.

Emily rushed to her mother and glared at Beto as he made a run for the back door. She raised her gun and squeezed off rounds until the gun was empty.

"Why? Why would you do that?" Emily asked. She grabbed her phone and dialed 911.

"This is Officer Emily Bebout. There's been a shooting at 66 Crag Lane. Woman, sixty-three years of age—cancer patient—with a GSW to the abdomen. Send an ambulance immediately!" She hung up and tossed the phone aside.

Stefanie fell onto her side, her blood spilling and pooling on the floor. Emily knelt and lifted her mother's upper body into her lap, pressing down hard on the wound. She ran shaking, bloody fingers through her mother's hair, and Stefanie reached a hand up, grabbed Emily's shirt, and squeezed. Tears poured from her eyes, seemingly forced out by the pain that pulled her face into a tightened expression.

"Hang on, Mom. Help is on the way."

"No," Stefanie said and coughed blood. Emily did her best to wipe it away and keep her mother clean. The effort was pointless, but in the moment that fact was lost on Emily.

"Why did you do that? He was looking to exchange you for his kid. It was a solution to get you back and then work on the gang once he had no leverage left."

"The answer is simple, and it may be hard for you accept, but . . . I wanted this."

Emily stiffened. "What? Why would you want this?"

"The cancer, Emily. I haven't been completely honest with you or your sister."

Tears welled in Emily's eyes. She moved her mother closer and increased pressure on the wound.

"The doctors have given me less than a month to live. I can't take the pain. It is so bad I can't face what is to come. This was my way out. My way of stepping aside so I can allow you to do your job and not worry about me."

"Oh my God," Emily said and rocked her mother. "You have so much to live for, Mom."

"No, I don't. The cancer has taken that away from me, and I'm so afraid of it. I don't want the pain. I know what it can do to a person. I can feel it growing inside me."

"Hannah is pregnant, Mom. You're going to be a grandmother."

Eyes that cried tears of pain momentarily turned off. Those words allowed joy to take over her face, but only for a moment. Her mouth again tightened as she tried to cope with the pain. Despite an attempt at a smile of satisfaction and pride, her expression couldn't hide the hurt. Emily could do nothing but watch and wait for help to arrive. Every second felt like a lifetime as her mother's life bled out. Every second added to her despair. Her anger. Her need for revenge.

"That's great," Stefanie said and managed another smile, her attempt at trying to comfort her daughter. "Grandma. That sounds wonderful, doesn't it?" Stefanie coughed.

Blood flew out of her mouth and sprayed Emily. She didn't flinch. She kept on stroking her mother's hair. She looked at her mother with the love of a daughter, her heart breaking, shattering into a million pieces. Emily knew what was coming. Right here in her arms, helpless to prevent it, death would come and take another mother. Rip her from her grasp and leave a void so gaping there wasn't anything but her anger big enough to fill it.

"It does sound lovely," Emily said and continued to stroke her mother's hair. "I don't know what to say, Mom."

"Tell me you love me and that you're going to look after your sister and that baby."

"I will, Mom. I promise."

Stefanie coughed. More blood. Her body stiffened with pain.

"I'm sorry, I just couldn't face the cancer anymore."

"I understand," Emily said even though she didn't. She had so much to live for. She could've fought it.

There, in Emily's arms Stefanie's breathing became shallow.

All the blood her mother had lost pooled around them. Stefanie coughed, gasped, and faded, her body limp, her suffering no more.

"Mom?" Emily squeezed her and shook her gently. "Mom?" Her body was soft, now free of the stiffening grasp of cancer. "Mom, no, don't leave us again!"

CHAPTER 28

regrouping

OUT OF BREATH and moving as fast as he could, Beto hurdled a wooden fence, fell to the ground, stood, and ran again, then slowed to scale a chain-link fence. He had somehow made it through a hail of gunfire that splintered wood and whizzed past his head, without being hit.

Unsure if Emily was in pursuit, he hurried through the yard. He was startled by the sound of a small dog barking at him. The fence, the dog, and his heavy breathing were all things to let Emily know exactly where he was. His fear forced his legs to move him faster. He gasped for air and tackled another fence, flipping over the top and spilling onto the ground, tired but determined to get away.

His attempt to escape had become so desperate that he failed to exit through the latched gate right next to him. He scrambled to his feet and hurried to a waiting vehicle. He ran to the passenger side and jumped through the open window.

"Go!"

He righted himself and pounded the dashboard.

"*¡Dije que vamos ahora!*"

Ernesto was behind the wheel, and he made haste, pressing heavily on the gas pedal, but not so much that the tires squealed.

"What the hell happened?" Ernesto asked as his eyes volleyed back and forth between Beto and the road.

"Just drive," Beto said, gasping for air, dripping with sweat.

The sounds of distant sirens approached. Adrenaline shook Beto's hands, and he felt nauseous. He looked at Ernesto, but Stefanie's wide eyes haunted him.

He saw movement in the back seat, and Vicki looked back at him with a swollen, purple face. He turned and saw fresh cuts covered by cheap band-aids; proof of a vicious beating at the hands of some unknown attacker. Her eyes were mere slits from the swelling. Red and purple lumps raised the skin on her forearms.

"What the hell happened to you?"

Vicki moved her eyes into her lap and licked her fat lips. "That cop, one of the twins, she came back in her civvies, just like you said she would. She was wearing a hooded sweatshirt, sweatpants; bitch tried to act like she was one of us. She knocked on the door and came at me hard. I was Tased and beaten with a damn nightstick. She kicked me so many times in the ribs that I can't breathe. You didn't tell me she was going to do that."

"I didn't think she had it in her."

"She's pissed."

"But you made it through it, and you still were mindful enough to send her to me. You did good, Vicki." Beto faced forward. "You did real good."

"She needs to pay for what she's done to Vicki," Ernesto said.

"The car. Where did you get it?"

"The cop's sister."

"What else is going on? Have you heard from Mateo?"

Ernesto looked out the side window, and his hands climbed all around the steering wheel. He watched the road and then sighed. "They were all killed in the raid on the precinct."

"Damn." Beto sat back. "This is a really big mess. I just killed the cop's mother right in front of her."

Quiet crept inside the vehicle, the rubber on the road the only sound.

"We can't even take you to a doctor," Beto said to Vicki. "I'm sorry, but you're going to need to endure."

"I don't need a doctor. You killing her mother . . . that's all the medicine I need for now. I hope that bitch that did this to me is suffering."

"¿Cómo?" Ernesto asked.

"She turned on me. Charged me. Tried to grab my gun."

"Your face?"

"Her fingernails."

"It looks bad."

Beto glanced in the mirror. "That's not even a concern. I've lost my leverage. The only way I know how to get my son back."

"Our son."

Beto didn't acknowledge Vicki's statement.

"I have an idea how you can get him back."

Beto looked at Ernesto.

"I'm listening."

"It'll require all of us. You, me, Vicki, Sandra, Santiago, Chino, and Manny."

"Santiago was shot. I don't want him becoming a liability."

"He refuses to be left out of the fight. He promises he's good to go."

"What are you thinking?"

"Sinners being Sinners. Let him sin as we sin."

Beto smiled. "Sinners sinning Southside style."

"There's no holding back," Ernesto said. "If this is going to work, we're only going to get one shot at this."

"Then let's get together with the others. We'll discuss your plan."

Ernesto picked up his phone and dialed out. "I have Beto. We're on our way."

CHAPTER 29

grieving and revenge

OFFICER MICHAEL DARIUS held Hannah by the bicep and escorted her past the group of scattered police officers busy toiling with the aftermath of Emily's showdown with Beto. Lights from multiple cruisers danced in the shadow of falling daylight.

Everyone was on edge. Anger and sadness spread across Emily's lawn. A sea of unknown, sorrowful faces dotted the path to the house, but Hannah just wanted them to return to wherever they came from.

The officers all wore bulletproof vests and carried high-powered weapons in harnesses; their fingers wrapped the triggers. Ample protection against what had been used against them before.

Silence thickened the outside air; every man and woman dressed in blue was a sentinel. There were no smiles. No, there was just the invisible weight of something bad, unavoidable and unshakable. An inevitable collision. Something bigger than all of this.

"What am I going to see, Michael?" Hannah asked.

Officer Darius continued to move her along as if he were trying to move faster than the sadness that chased them.

"I'm not sure," he said, the lie obvious. "I didn't go inside," he said, still fibbing.

"Emily?"

"She's inside."

Hannah pulled away from her escort and hurried up the front steps. She opened the door and rushed into the house. In the center of the kitchen was a body covered with a white, bloodstained sheet. Emily

124

was on the couch about ten feet away, alone and staring, fixated on the bloody lump, not acknowledging her sister's arrival. Hannah saw that Emily's clothes had been stained with blood, too, her torso, arms, and face dressed in red war paint.

Now she noticed the shock in Emily's stare and the quiet anger in the clench of her jaw.

Hannah looked at her feet. It was the only way to escape the devastation she'd stepped into. Yet deep down inside she knew there was no escaping this and everything that had been. Trent, the wheelchair dummy, and the memories from her childhood; avoidance was a reaction of complete denial to try and help preserve her sanity. But she couldn't just curl up and shrink away. She needed to be the strong one for once. Strong for her baby and her sister.

Hannah focused on her twin, trying to ignore the blood and the dead body of the woman who had done so much for her and her sister, and to push aside the need to fall to her knees and weep forever.

"Emily?" she said, her voice timid.

The call broke the spell Emily was under, and she slowly lifted her head and found Hannah with her eyes. She looked at the blood on her hands, her clothing, and then at her mother. She was in shock.

"It looks like I've been painting," Emily said. "That's what I've been thinking. That all of this is a painting. That's kind of weird to be thinking, but that's what I'm thinking. That I'm looking at a painting. The kind that confuses you when you look at it. It's the inevitable tragedy that is somehow our life. A family curse. Mom, Dad, Uncle Glenn, Officer Buckley and his wife, Trent, and now Mom again. How does someone lose their mother twice? That's not supposed to happen."

Hannah hurried to Emily and hugged her tightly. "What did they do?"

Emily remained limp in Hannah's hold. "It was Beto. He shot her."

Hannah couldn't hold back the tears. They came hard, and she whimpered. She could hear Emily's voice speaking words to be strong, but the words she said were muffled and forced. It was like Hannah was underwater—her sister's words garbled and fading into the abyss as she sank farther and farther, becoming something else in the darkening distance.

Knowing that the Sinners killed their mother and did this—whatever her sister was becoming—tore deeply at Hannah. They only had each other now, and Hannah didn't want to fade away. She hugged her sister tighter, but still, Emily remained limp in her arms.

"I'm so sorry," Hannah said, and her eyes drifted to their mother.

"I am, too," Emily said, so far away. "I couldn't save her. It happened so fast."

"This is not your fault!"

Hannah's gaze moved away from her mother's covered body, and she looked at her sister. But Emily just stared into the distance.

"Emily?"

"It was Beto. He shot her right in front of me."

"I know," Hannah said and wiped her tears. "You just told me that."

Emily looked at Hannah, her jaw tight, her hands curled into fists. "Beto did this!"

"They've taken almost everything from us. I'm trying to resist what I'm feeling. I know how hard it is. Please, don't let them take you too."

"I can still hear the gunshot. I froze and saw the look on Mom's face. I'm not sure why, but I just stood there frozen, looking. I hesitated long enough for Beto to get away."

"How did this happen?"

"Mom did it," Emily said. "She made Beto shoot her."

"Wait. What?"

Hannah sat, reality fading into the idea of what Emily said. The scenario played out in her mind, and she rejected it with a shiver.

"She turned on him, grabbed for his gun. There was no chance she'd be able to get that from him, and she knew it. She had to know that. She admitted to knowing that."

"Maybe she did it because she was trying to protect you?"

"No," Emily said and shook her head.

"Then why?"

"You should've seen the way she moved. All stiff and slow. As she lay there on the floor in my lap, gasping for air, she confessed to me."

"What did she confess, Emily?"

"That she wanted to die. That she didn't tell us the cancer had gotten really aggressive and the doctors didn't give her a month to live. I think she said a month."

"Why wouldn't she—"

"Because she didn't want us to worry. But she figured this, here, that it would bring closure to what was supposed to happen with Beto all those years back. I think she felt when she put an empty gun to his head and pulled the trigger, he should've killed her right there. The time she had was borrowed. That it would be the way it was supposed to be. She said she was afraid of the cancer. She didn't want to deal with the pain. Beto was her way out." Emily allowed herself a moment to gather her thoughts. "I don't know. There's so many different ways to interpret her actions. Suicide by thug."

"My God," Hannah said. "Why wouldn't she tell us? Maybe we could've helped her."

"Yeah, maybe." Emily took another moment. Her face contorted into something wicked. "If I kill his kid, then we'll be even."

Hannah shook her head, went to her knees, and took her sister's hands. "No." She squeezed. "No, Emily, don't think like that, and don't talk like that! This is not eye for an eye."

"His son is all he cares about. That's how I get him back for what he's done to us. So he can feel what we feel."

"No," Hannah said again and stood. "Look at me."

Emily didn't, so Hannah took her sister by the hand again and held it with a firm grasp.

"Don't you understand it'll never end?" Hannah said. "This is a cycle our family is caught up in with these people. You know what we do to get out of it? We don't engage with them anymore. We mourn and focus on the positives we have left in our lives." Hannah looked at her mother's covered body. "I didn't get a chance to say goodbye. I will have to live with that." She stopped to wipe away her tears and gather herself, unsure how much strength she had left. "But I want us to move on."

"She told me to tell you that she loves you."

Hannah cried again and slumped forward, nearly broken down. When she steadied her breathing, Hannah said, "We mourn her death and leave here. We start over again. Forget this place. Forget wanting to get revenge. It makes us no better than them if we do."

"I can't do that because they've made me no better," Emily said. "I can be no better than the revenge I need to get. I can't live with the anger in my heart. I'm broken and dangerous."

"You are better than revenge and can live with everything that's happened. You're upset, and I'm upset. You're in shock. But I need you." She placed Emily's hand on her belly. "I need help with my baby."

"You're going to be a great mother, Hannah. If you have a girl—"

"Emily Stefanie Bebout."

Emily cracked a smile. "That's a beautiful name. I wish Mom and Dad were here to see the baby when she's born."

"Me too."

"Or he."

Hannah laughed through the tears. "Yes, or he."

"Do you have the gun I gave you?"

Hannah stared at Emily.

"Do you have it?"

"Yes."

Emily became stern. "Safety off. Have it on you at all times. Bathroom. Shower. Supermarket. Wherever you go and whatever you're doing. Do you understand?"

"They've assigned Officer Darius to me."

"He's a good officer, Hannah, but I want you to listen to me. Do you understand? They'll kill him given the chance. They'll kill him to get to you. Do you get that?"

"Yes."

"Promise me."

"I promise."

"We're not going to want to be in here while they finish with the crime scene. I can't bear to see them photographing her. This house has become nothing more than a morgue."

"Let's leave then," Hannah said, trying to be strong. She pulled on Emily's hand. "Come on, let's go outside. Let's get away from here."

The sisters left the house, and neither one of them looked at the body of their mother again. They held onto each other and tried to put on their bravest faces as they walked through the sea of faceless officers and first responders who offered words of condolences that they couldn't even hear.

"Emily?"

Officer Darius stepped in front of her, and Emily stopped.

"Can I have a word with you?"

"Sure."

"Alone?"

Emily rubbed her sister's back and stepped away.

WHEN THEY HAD walked enough distance that Hannah couldn't overhear, Officer Darius spoke. "Creighton wants you to take your sister and get out of town."

"No way, I'm not going anywhere."

"I don't think the captain was requesting."

"My sister can go—I'm not. I'll arrange for someone to come and get my sister. A friend or something. Someone I know that'll care for her. She'll be in a safe place where the Sinners could never find her. I have someone in mind."

"The captain—"

"I'll talk to the captain after I get Hannah out of harm's way."

Emily stepped away from Darius and made a phone call on her cell.

"Hey."

She listened.

"I know it has been a while. I'm sorry."

She listened again.

"Can we meet up and I'll fill you in? It's too much to do on the phone right now."

She listened.

"I know it has been all over the news. And yes, that's where we'll be. Can you give us an hour before you come?"

She listened and switched the phone from one ear to the other.

"Thank you so much," Emily said. "I can't tell you how much this means to me."

Emily hung up the phone and returned to where Hannah was waiting. She took her by the arm and led her away.

"C'mon, let's go."

"Where are we going?"

"For a ride. There's something I think we need to do. We should've done it a long time ago."

"What is it?"

"You'll see."

CHAPTER 30

organized

VICKI, CHINO, ERNESTO, Manny, and Beto stood behind an abandoned building on the outskirts of town. A van with the back doors ajar revealed a stockpile of weapons and body armor.

Chino reached in and passed around automatic weapons and extra ammo already loaded into clips.

"Like the raid on the precinct," Beto said. "Ernesto's plan may come with a price. I think it's the only option we have at our disposal. Sinners sinning. That's what we do. We've waited long, and we've already made a permanent impression. We're all in. This is our chance to get everyone to fear the Sinners once again."

"Those who don't will learn," Ernesto said. "They've disrespected you and the club. This can't go unanswered or unfinished."

"There is a price to pay for crossing us," Manny said.

"This is a great day," Chino said and pulled the lever back on his AK-47. The click-click of the weapon sounded like snapping teeth from an aggressive, rabid animal.

"Does everyone know exactly what must be done?" Beto said.

"Mayhem."

"Sinning."

"Southside style."

Beto took a bulletproof vest from the van and put it on. "We all wear one. Ski masks to cover your faces. Don't take them off. Not ever. The slim chance you get to escape . . . this piece of fabric is the only thing you have to keep someone from identifying you or not."

Everyone put on their vests. They pulled the ski masks over the tops of their heads, but not over their faces just yet.

"The element of surprise is our greatest ally. Torment and intimidation are the goals here. Distract. Redirect. Let's stay in control."

"We got this."

"Understood, amigo."

"I'm going to take the car," Beto said and slapped Ernesto's back. "You guys are getting the van. Be noisy. Make a grand entrance. *Buena suerte.*"

One by one they embraced with a hug and a special handshake. Vicki kissed Beto and rubbed the side of his face. "You know what to do."

"It's already done as far as I'm concerned."

They hugged again and broke apart. "I hope to see you all back here soon," Beto said to the group.

Vicki, Ernesto, Manny, and Chino piled into the van and drove away.

Beto watched the vehicle kick up dirt and fade into the distance. He hurried into the car. They only had a small window of opportunity, so he made haste. He placed the gun on the seat beside him and stuck to the side roads as much as possible. His destination was only a few miles away.

Oddly, he was nervous. And for the first time in a long time, he had a measure of doubt as to whether or not this would work—but he was running out of options.

CHAPTER 31

home sweet home

EMILY DROVE DOWN a street familiar to both her and Hannah. Although the details of this place had long ago faded, a sense of knowing and foreboding sat in the backseat and kept them company.

Hannah looked out the passenger side window and intently examined the large houses with fancy cars parked in the long driveways as they drove past. What she saw screamed money. If any of these people ever found themselves in her position, even they wouldn't have enough money and toys to pay off the one thing that made everyone even in this life: death. *Money gives you power*, she thought darkly, *but death makes everyone equal in the end.*

"Why are we here?" Hannah said.

"It has been far too long. I think it's time to face this and put this ghost behind us."

EMILY ROLLED UP on a house set back far from the road and pulled into the driveway. It ended at a dormant, moss-covered fountain in the center of a roundabout. The last time Emily remembered seeing the fountain, the water within was frozen solid and the vehicle they'd exited had been dented by an aggressive woman now long dead. The house had been overtaken by the foliage that had covered the siding in its tight tendril grip. It looked like a huge gift-wrapped box. It might as well have been Pandora's Box, though, and it should never be opened again.

Emily shut off the engine and exited the car. She stared at her childhood home, and Hannah followed, settling into step beside her sister.

"It feels strange being here," Emily said.

"Too sentimental to be sold but too painful to visit," Hannah said.

"It has been a long time."

"I'm surprised no one has complained about how it looks."

Emily looked down the long driveway at the large bushes and the thick row of trees that did a great job of concealing the aging, uncared for house that was once a home.

"It serves as a reminder to so many people about what happened; what gave the town the nickname Battleground. I think they want it here . . . like this."

Emily jingled a set of keys.

"I don't want to go in," Hannah said.

"You don't have to. I do."

Emily slid the key into the door. The lock was stiff and required her to work the key back and forth before the tumblers let go of their long hold.

She pushed the door open.

The hinges protested with a loud creak. A waft of stale air rushed out of the house and blasted Emily in the face. It smelt of stillness and bad memories that had been sealed away. Maybe she should've left it undisturbed.

"I'll be back in a little bit," Emily said over her shoulder, ignoring what her mind was telling her. She stepped into the house, and it was like going back in time. Everything was exactly as it had been twenty years ago.

Hannah came inside, grabbed Emily's arm, and clung to her. A tremble coursed through her body and into Emily's.

"It's OK," Emily said and moved farther into the house, leading her sister along. The furniture and floors were covered with a thick layer of dust, and cobwebs strung from corners of the high ceilings. The large, sweeping staircase remained a path to one of the worst memories they carried around. Upstairs was where their mother had committed suicide.

Downstairs, not too far from where they stood, was the long hallway where their uncle Glenn played monster with them. The shouts of joy were faint and only in Emily's mind, but they were fond.

"You remember hanging onto his legs and sitting on his feet?"

"I can feel it," Hannah said and smiled. "The monster that sniffed the air to find us."

"I think I wanted to come here to make peace with the tragedies from our childhood."

Hannah nodded. "It was a good idea. Remembering things that weren't horrible about our childhood is good."

"I couldn't think of any other way. But come on, let's look into the past we've forbidden ourselves to come to terms with."

The memory of their father, exactly where they stood now, was where he sat in the wheelchair with his head flopped to the side, spittle running out of his mouth. His greatness and kind, giving soul were trapped inside a body that no longer worked. He was a perfect gift to the world that had been destroyed before it was ever opened.

Tears flowed as they hugged, and Emily gently pulled away. "I think I've seen enough."

Hannah nodded. "Yeah, me too."

They exited the house and locked the door to forever seal away the pain of their past. Neither one of them wanted to look back at the giant dark memory but would rather leave it behind to crumble.

They got into the vehicle, turned around the fountain, and exited the driveway. Emily drove down the street, pulled the car to the curb, and leaned back in her seat with a heavy sigh.

She reached out and touched her sister.

"You're not coming home with me."

"What are you talking about?" Hannah said, alarmed.

"What's going on with the Sinners is no place for an expecting mother. They're after you to weaken me like they did with Mom. If you don't want to go, to help me look after you the best way I know how, then I ask you to consider the baby and the risk you'd be putting your child in. From the moment of conception that baby became your first and only priority."

"No, Emily, we need to stick together. We need to look out for each other."

"Yes, we do. This is my looking out for you and your looking out for me. This is the best way I know how."

A car pulled up behind them, and a very large older man got out. Hannah turned in the seat and watched the man approach the car.

"Do you remember hearing the stories about the butcher? The man that wrote the license plate number down on a foam plate and gave it to Mom?"

"Vaguely."

"This is him. His name is Eddie DePina."

"OK. Why is he here?"

Eddie arrived at the driver's side window. Emily rolled it down. "Thank you for coming on such short notice."

"I told your aunt . . ." He looked away, down the block toward the house they'd just left with sad tears that bubbled to the surface. "I mean your mother . . . that whenever she needed me, I'd be there for her. That meant the both of you too. Whatever she or you two needed I would give or do if it was within my power. We kept in touch, and she never once asked for anything other than friendly talk. I've been watching the news, and I see the Sinners are active once again."

"They killed our mother."

"What?" Eddie said and stood upright. His eyes brightened, and he seemed unsteady on his feet. "How?" he asked softly.

"She was shot and killed only a few hours ago."

Eddie held onto the car, and his focus sank within. "My God."

"Will you take my sister with you? She's pregnant and needs to be away from here. Away from them."

"Yes, of course, I told your mother . . . I can't believe she's . . ."

"I know." Emily looked at Hannah. "Mr. DePina will take care of you."

"You've got my word," he said. "I won't let anything happen to you."

"He's going to take you away from here until this is sorted out."

Hannah shook her head and watched Eddie walk around the car and to the passenger side. "I remember him," she whispered.

He opened the door. "Come," he said. "It's what's best for you and your unborn baby."

He extended a hulking hand that showed years of hard work. Hannah looked at Emily, and Emily said, "I will come to you when this is done."

Hannah sat in contemplation, but soon her hand went to her belly and rested there. She hugged her sister hard and turned and accepted Eddie's hand. She exited the vehicle, and he escorted her to his car.

Emily watched them in the rearview mirror as Eddie helped Hannah into the passenger seat and walked around to the driver's side of his car and waved at Emily.

He got into the car and drove away. Emily didn't wait. She headed directly back to the precinct.

CHAPTER 32

wedding crashers

THE SUN BEAT down on the blacktop and distorted the air, making it shimmer. The day vibrated with a palpable nervousness.

A white van crawled down the street; evil intent sat within the belly of the box. Chino, Ernesto, and Manny were in the back, and Vicki was behind the wheel, looking in the rearview.

"You guys ready?"

"Oh, we're ready."

The vehicle came to a slow stop in front of a reception hall. The men held their automatic weapons against their padded chests, pulled their ski masks over their faces, kicked the back doors open, and piled out.

They slammed the doors shut, and Manny pounded on the steel door, prompting Vicki to speed away. Like a well-trained task force, the men descended upon the building, warding off any bystanders that watched them approach the wedding hall by pointing their weapons at them.

"Don't be a hero," Chino said.

"Go ahead and call the police, but get yourself far away first," Manny said.

They stopped at the door, and Manny pulled out a can of red spray paint and tagged the front doors with a large 'SS,' the ends forked with the devil's tail. He tossed the can aside, and they entered the wedding hall where a reception was going on.

People dressed in beautiful gowns and tuxedos were dancing to loud music on a small dance floor. No one noticed the gunmen as Chino hurried to the DJ, hit him with the butt of his gun, and turned the music off.

Everyone stopped and looked.

"Good afternoon, everyone," he said into the microphone. "I am a Sinner, and my friends and I have come to change your lives. Now, everyone needs to raise their hands as high up as they can reach. If you don't follow our instructions explicitly, you will find that we don't mind shooting people."

Everyone in the crowd raised their hands.

"That's good," he said. "See? We're off to a good start. Now we would like you all to lie facedown on the floor, but do it slowly. No sudden moves. No one here is a hero today. I hope I make myself clear."

The people went down to their knees and then to the floor. Ernesto and Manny watched every move they made, circling the gathering like vultures ready to pick the carcasses of their fallen prey.

A server came out of the back and dropped the platter she'd so eloquently balanced on her shoulder. Glass smashed on the floor, metal rattled, and food splattered. Chino hurried forward, grabbed the frightened woman, and forced her to the floor with the others. She quivered.

"No, no, no," Chino said, and the woman quieted.

"My friend is going to choose five of you," Chino said, pacing back and forth, the microphone to his mouth, his other hand wrapping the grip of the AK-47 and his finger hovering near the trigger. "That's right, the five of you will proceed to remove the cell phones from your pockets, and you will then dial 911. You'll be the chosen ones, YouTube sensations. Think of the book deals you'll get. The *20/20* interviews."

"You," Ernesto said and pushed the tip of his gun into the small of an older man's back. "You," to a young woman in her early twenties. "You and you," to a couple lying next to each other. "And you," he said to a young man.

"Go ahead and dial and tell them where you are and what is happening here. Tell them there are eight gunmen in here, and we are ready to kill you all if the child named Urban Daraio is not released into his father's custody."

The people dialed numbers on their phones. Some had steady hands, but most fumbled with their devices. They conveyed the message that Chino had ordered them to, and they remained on the line, awaiting further instructions.

Chino walked over to the young man. "What is your name?"

"Sean."

"Sean what?"

"Sean Donohue."

"Well, Sean Donohue, do you mind if I borrow your phone?"

"No," he said and held it out. "Of course not."

Chino took the phone with a smile, pressed it against his ear, and listened.

"Are you sure there are eight?" the voice on the other end of the phone asked.

"I'm sure there are eight," Chino said.

"Do they have weapons? Can you describe them?"

"AK-47. Bulletproof vests and ski masks."

"Who is this?"

"Me? I'm just a Sinner. And you are?"

"Nancy Lacey. What happened to the young man I was just talking to?"

"Well, Nancy Lacey, the woman with such a sweet, caring voice, Sean is doing just fine for now. He was kind enough to let me use his phone so I could talk to you."

"And who are you?"

Chino laughed. "You're not listening, Nancy. I've already told you that I'm a Sinner. One that believes in bloodshed to send a message. *Uno por muchos. Las vidas de estas personas dependen en su cooperación.*"

He took the phone away from his ear and held it in front of his face.

"I hope you understand what I'm saying or find a translator quickly."

He disconnected the call and placed the phone down in front of Sean. "Now go ahead and start video recording," he said. "In fact, all of you that have your phones out, I want you to keep recording until the phone won't let you record anymore. One at a time. When one stops, tell us, and someone else will record so everyone will know exactly what happened in here this day."

Chino knelt next to Sean and talked softly to him. "Film him," he said and pointed at Ernesto. Sean did as he was instructed.

Ernesto walked over to the bride and groom. "Stand up," he said. "Congratulations to both of you."

The couple stood, crying.

"You are free to go. Don't ask to stay or try to negotiate terms for your mom, dad, sister, or any of your relatives. They're staying here until this is all over. What I'm offering you now is our wedding gift to you, and you must take it."

The groom took his wife's hand and pulled her along, though she cried and shrieked in protest. They soon exited the reception hall.

"You see?" Chino said. "We're not unreasonable."

The sounds of many sirens grew nearer. The Sinners pulled their bolts back, and their guns clicked as they accepted a round into the chamber.

"Why don't we get this party started?" Manny said.

"That sounds like a wonderful plan," Chino said. "Time to start sinning."

"*Pecadores pecando*," Ernesto said. "This is what we do!"

"Sean," Chino said, and Sean looked at him. "Thank you for allowing me to use your phone."

Sean hesitated. "You're welcome."

Manny poked the server on the back. "And you, let's get the people out of the back. I feel much better as a tight little group. To anyone that thinks of doing anything other than exactly what we say—" he looked at Chino.

Chino moved the tip of his gun to Sean's forehead. "*Deberías estar orgulloso de ser el elegido, tu vida para los demás.*"

The sound of a single shot from an assault rifle rattled through the reception hall.

CHAPTER 33

into the teeth

THE RADIO CRACKLED to life in Emily's vehicle. "All units respond, we have a 10-28 in progress at Lombardo Reception Hall. Multiple hostages. Go in with 10-99."

Emily picked up her cell phone and hit a pre-programmed number. It rang twice.

"Hello?"

"Captain?"

"Emily?"

"I heard the call and need to come in."

"That's good. Come in and let the others handle this."

"This is a ruse, Captain."

"What?"

"This is just a ploy to get people to move one way while they move another."

"Maybe," Creighton said. "Whatever it is, we need to put an end to it, and fast. Enough people have been hurt. They attacked the precinct earlier, killing even more of us. These people are ruthless."

"I'm telling you, someone or many more of them are going to the precinct again. They're after the boy."

"He's in lockdown."

"I know, Captain. I know this is going to sound crazy, but you need to send everyone out. You need to make it look like they've fooled us."

"They've come in here and slaughtered my men and women. We're thin, and the people in that reception hall need our help. I called in the

Forest Hill Police Department to assist, but they're about twenty minutes out."

"That's OK."

"It's not OK."

"It is, because I know their plan. We can bait them. Beat them at their own game."

"Emptying out the precinct will never work," Creighton said, his voice at a shout through the phone. "Who in their right mind would think the precinct would be emptied after what happened here?"

"The Sinners would. They know how badly we want them. They think us desperate, but it's a double play."

"What do you mean?"

"They have hostages to exchange for the boy. This is a way to keep our limited resources tied up while we try to negotiate and someone else comes in behind them and tries to infiltrate again."

The phone went quiet.

"Captain?"

"Yeah, I'm here, Emily. What do you propose?"

Emily hit the gas and sped toward the precinct. Her plan was fleshed out within seconds of the question hitting her ear.

"It's like I said, send almost everyone out of the precinct. Divert the Forest Hill police and get them on scene at the reception hall too. The Sinners need to see a huge presence. I'm coming to you so we can hash out these plans."

"And then what?"

"We get these bastards for everything they've done. For every person that is grieving because of them."

"We're not going Wild, Wild West here, Emily. As much as we want to, we have to follow the law and try and take them in."

"Killing them would be too kind. I want to see them rot in prison for the rest of their lives. This is our chance to capture Beto and cripple the Sinners once and for all."

CHAPTER 34

officer down

BETO SAT IN the idling vehicle and watched the activity outside the police precinct from behind tinted windows. It had been more than fifteen minutes since everything had gone quiet. A dozen or more police cruisers had raced away, speeding in the direction of the reception hall.

Still, he thought the precinct would be teeming with police and crime scene investigators since the bloody shootout. But a need for revenge, apparently, took precedence over everything else—behavior it seemed Ernesto not only predicted but understood.

"You're a genius, Ernesto," Beto said to himself.

Their ploy was working. The cops wanted the Sinners, and they'd dispatched everyone to get them.

Kicking the car door open, Beto spilled into the street, hurried up the steps, and peeked through the glass door. The officer at the lobby desk departed with a handful of paperwork, oblivious to Beto's approach.

Beto swung the door open and stepped into the precinct. He felt his anger rise along with his adrenaline. How dare they bring his son to such a vile place! He remained still a moment and listened. The quiet was invasive, distracting almost, but the ring of an unanswered phone in the back was promising. It was time to go.

He moved with caution. His AK-47 held tightly against his vested chest and the backup .45 and Glock stuffed into his waistband were assurances that his infiltration, if interrupted, would be met with extreme resistance. This was a father protecting his child, and all rules—if there were any to begin with—were gone. They disappeared the moment the police took his boy. Beto was driven by the need to get his son back by any means necessary.

He pressed his back against the wall so no one could come up behind him. He made his way into the hallway behind the lobby, using stealth and quick looks to see who was where, his hearing tuned in for anyone who might be approaching.

The hallway was clear. He walked into the main section of the precinct, which was a wide-open office where dozens of desks had been strewn throughout. But yellow tape, bullet holes, and broken and displaced things were still scattered throughout the battle-scarred room.

His men had created this chaos, and he smiled deep within—but the pounding of his nervous heart didn't allow that feeling of accomplishment to stay for too long.

"I think we need to get the state police here too," a man said from somewhere out of sight. "We're vulnerable."

"McGonigal?"

"Yes, Captain?"

Beto heard muffled muttering as the response.

"I'll do that. Thank you, Captain," McGonigal said at the far end of the room Beto was in. A door tapped shut.

Beto hid behind one of the few partitions that remained upright. He listened to Officer McGonigal's passing footsteps and happened a glance. The officer's back was to him, and he was oblivious to Beto's presence. McGonigal, it seemed, was talking to himself, his nose buried in a clipboard and his other hand grasping a cup of coffee as he returned to the front desk. His troubled mind was palpable—like something wounded—and it helped feed Beto's bravery. He stood and moved forward.

Logic told Beto the holding rooms would be in the opposite direction from where the officer had just come. But Beto needed something before he could move forward with his plans and would have to strike the moment the opportunity presented itself.

Beto watched the officer disappear into the front of the precinct, resuming his post behind the front desk. He followed but remained cautious to stay undetected.

"Repeat, all units converge on the Lombardo hall. The Sinners are there, and they have a room full of hostages," the officer said into his radio and placed the clipboard and cup of coffee down. "Officer Bebout to channel three."

Beto froze at the mention of that name. Maybe he could get one of the sisters too . . .

McGonigal flipped through radio channels, took off the keys that were clipped on his belt loop, and unlocked a filing cabinet to his right.

"This is Emily," her voice crackled through the radio.

McGonigal flinched. "Damn," he said to himself and depressed the button on the radio. "Emily, Cap wants to know how far out you are."

"ETA is about two minutes."

"He wants you to take lead on negotiations. You know those bastards like no one else. Make sure none of the civilians are harmed, and most of all, keep everyone in blue safe. We've lost too many already."

"Copy that," she responded, her tone biting.

McGonigal sighed, ran stiff fingers through his hair, and tipped the cup of coffee, its contents spilling into the open cabinet. "Damn it!"

"What is it, McGonigal?"

"Nerves, Emily. Sorry, didn't realized I'd pressed the call button. Just fumbling around here."

"You OK?"

"I'm good. Everything is eerily quiet here."

"We can trade places."

"No thanks."

"Didn't think so. Over and out."

McGonigal exited the office on the opposite side from which he had entered, leaving his keys on the countertop. Beto hurried forward, grabbed the keys, and wasted no time moving through the hallway, going the opposite direction of where he was before. He came upon a line of rooms. He went to the first room and tried the keys. After a tense minute of searching, he found the one that worked and opened the door. He took a single step into the room, allowing his gun to lead the way. It was empty.

He went to the second door and fumbled through the large ring of keys, trying each one, muttering under his breath, "C'mon."

He looked behind himself to make sure no one was coming. Then the lock gave way and the door swung open. His son stared at him, and he at his son down the barrel of his AK-47.

Beto lowered his weapon. "Urban!"

"Dad!"

EMILY SPIED BETO through the crack in the door behind him. She watched him gain access to the room Urban was held in and looked over her shoulder at Frerk. "He's in," she whispered. "He's got an automatic, Kevlar, and some back-up pistols."

"Bum-rush him?"

"Not yet," Emily said. "Let him think he has this. He has to find the key to unlock the cuffs binding his brat to the table."

"Good luck with that."

"Yeah," Emily said and smiled. "It's so good to see this. Removing that key from the ring almost seems unfair."

"Let me have a look, would ya?"

Emily stepped aside, and Frerk had a look.

"He's trying the keys now," he said.

"I'm sorry," Emily said as she quickly grabbed Frerk from behind, her forearm coiled around his neck. He used his hands to try to peel her grip away, but it was locked in place.

Frerk soon went limp in her grasp, and she lay him down on the floor. "I'm sorry, friend, but this is between me and him."

Emily took Frerk's sidearm and tucked it into the back of her utility belt. She held her own sidearm out and exited the room, her weapon centered on Beto's skull. Ignorant to Emily's approach, he toiled trying to find the key that would free his son, who was shackled to a stainless-steel table with a loop on the top.

"The key's not on there," Emily said, and Beto turned, eyes wide. He stumbled backward and fumbled for his gun. Emily clasped her weapon with both hands and continued to move forward. "I wouldn't do that."

Beto steadied himself, eyeing his son.

Emily kept her weapon trained on Beto and pressed her back against the wall, hiding her backup weapon as she retreated to the rear of the room. She motioned to Beto with a twist of her wrist.

"Shut the door," she said.

She settled into a chair in the corner of the room and smiled. Beto paused, apparently in contemplation.

"I wouldn't do whatever it is you're thinking you can do. You're not that fast, and I'm a hell of a shot," she said. "Now, kick the door shut. It seems we have ourselves a dilemma here."

"There's no dilemma," Beto said and closed the door, moving so his hands stayed clear of his gun. "I've come to take my son, and then I'm gone. You'll never see me again."

"Let me get this straight. You think I'm going to just let you take your son and allow you to walk away? Leave you whole and fulfilled when I'm so broken and empty?"

"Yes. If you want the killings to stop, it's the only way."

"You think I'm going to just forget about what you did to my mother? To all of the people in this precinct? To the people at that wedding reception?"

"The people inside that reception hall are nothing more than a diversion so I can get my son," Beto said. "They're not going to harm anyone unless I say something has gone wrong here. They're ordered to stall long enough to give me enough time to get my son, and then they're going to give themselves up without a fight."

"God, I hope not. A fight would give us a good chance to get rid of the scum that taints this town." Emily stared hard. "That includes you, Beto. Scum, that's what you are."

"So, you expected me to come here?"

"I baited you, as you thought you were baiting us," Emily said. "But the good guys always win."

"So there's a team ready to storm into this room and attempt to keep me from my son?"

"Yes, that's supposed to be the plan . . . but there's so much unfinished business between us." Emily pointed at the chair in the opposite corner of the room. "Take that chair there. I want you to tilt it back and put it under the doorknob. Then stand on the chair. That'll buy us enough time to finish this."

Beto laughed. "You have this all figured out, don't you?"

"You have no idea."

Beto took the chair and wedged it underneath the door handle. He stood on the chair and it locked into place.

"We don't have to go through this," Beto said and stepped down. "All I want is my son, and you'll never see me again."

"Your son is staying here with us. If he ever stands a chance, he needs to stay away from you."

Urban started to cry. "Dad, I'm scared."

"Everything is going to be OK," Beto said. "*Mantenerte fuerte.*"

"There's nothing more you can do, Beto. You're trapped in this room with your child and with the demon you helped create. He could fall victim to the gunfire meant for his father. You do understand that I want you dead, don't you? I know that is the only way this will end."

"You're not going to shoot me. And I'm not leaving without him. You do understand that, don't you?"

"Dad?" Urban said.

"You're not leaving at all," Emily said. "I already told you that I intended on killing you."

"Dad?"

Beto raised a hand, silencing his son. "You're going to do this in front of my child?"

"You did it in front of my mother's child," Emily said with a stone face. "That's a hard thing to get over . . . to try and comprehend . . . to get out of your head."

"It was an accident."

"Whatever it was, it brought us here to settle this bad blood for good. Now raise your weapon."

"Dad, don't do this!"

"There's no other way," Beto said and moved quick. He grabbed his weapon and raised it. The room exploded in sound.

Blam!

Emily rocked back in the chair, the weapon flew from her grasp, her arms flailed, and she fell from the chair. On her knees, she gasped for air and aimed her weapon up. Beto stepped toward her.

Crash!

Beto looked as the door bowed, but the chair held. He turned his attention back to Emily, who was collapsed chest over her knees, moaning, her rounded back facing him as she took measured breaths.

"Dad, she has a—"

"Get up!" he shouted. "I hit you in the vest, and you're not that good a shot. I spared you so I can use you as a shield. You're my ticket to getting out of here."

"OK," Emily said and slowly uncurled. Her voice carried the sound of agony as she did so.

"WHAT THE HELL is she doing?" Creighton said. "I knew I shouldn't have let her do this!"

Three officers dressed in full assault clothing stood behind him and watched a monitor.

"Go, now!" the captain said. "Go, go, go!"

The two men and one woman hurried toward the room. The biggest of the bunch ran at the door and hit it. The officer bounced off the door like it was made of brick and lost his balance.

The other officers moved forward and took turns trying to kick the door in.

EMILY SQUEEZED THE trigger and hit Beto in the leg. Blood from torn flesh sprayed the room, and he spun and fell to the floor, dropping the AK-47. He regained his composure, grabbed his .45, and aimed it at Emily, hers centered on him.

"On three," Emily said with a sinister grin. "This is the way it ends."

"Not like this. Not in front of my kid."

"He needs to see what will happen to him if he follows the path you've shown him. He needs to know that no matter how much he tries to intimidate people that there will always be someone like me that will be brave enough to stand up to people like you."

"No."

Emily's smile widened, and she laughed maniacally. She held her weapon steady.

"On three. One . . . two . . ."

CHAPTER 35

the love of a mother

VICKI EASED THE van to the side of the road. She parked a half a block away from the precinct, keeping the eerily inactive building in view. She leaned her head against the padded headrest and sighed.

The role she was supposed to play in the day's events was clear: Return to the same place they departed from and wait for Beto to arrive with Urban. She was to remain out of harm's way in case things started to go south. This would ensure Urban had a parent to go to once he got out of the system.

But it didn't feel right. Nothing about the plan felt right. The more she thought about it, it seemed too simple to lure so many people in one direction from another highly sensitive location. Why would they leave her child unguarded? The question pounded in her mind. Why, especially when he was the reason for all of this?

Yes, she saw all of the police cruisers blasting by her as she doubled back. Their red and blue lights blinked wildly, and their sirens wailed.

"They know he's coming. They're setting him up," she muttered aloud to herself.

She raised her head and watched the precinct again. Another ailing thought consumed her: *I wonder if Urban is even inside? If he is, what if he needs me?* With mixed feelings of foreboding and rogue maternal courage, Vicki exited the vehicle and stormed toward the precinct, gun in hand.

CHAPTER 36

cultures collide

BLAM!

Beto jerked.

Blam!

Emily shouted out. The room filled with blue smoke and Urban's screams.

"Dad!"

Emily was on her back, looking at the ceiling. The lights above dimmed in her vision; a sign death was upon her, she had no doubt. She gasped for air and wondered if this was how badly her mother hurt when Beto shot her.

"What did you do to my father!"

Smash!

The door finally gave way, and the three officers, along with Captain Creighton, stormed into the room.

"Get him out of here!" Creighton shouted.

Beto had taken a bullet to the neck. Emily had taken one to the face.

The officers quickly took stock of the room. Beto was dead. Emily clung to life. Barely.

Creighton knelt next to Emily, and he held her.

"Why did you do this?" he asked, visibly upset.

"Because I couldn't live with the pain anymore," she wanted to say but gurgled instead. There was so much liquid. Thick and in her throat and lungs. She could taste it and smell it too. Knew she was drowning in it. She wanted to grab Creighton back, feel that he was there until she wasn't. But numbness had settled in, and she couldn't feel anything but the cold. That, and the blackness she reached to touch. It was finally over.

CHAPTER 37

what a reception

EVERYONE SCREAMED AT the sound of the gunfire and the grotesque explosion of young Sean Donohue's head breaking open from the point-blank execution shot.

"A message," Chino said.

"Everyone, settle down," Ernesto said.

"Two will be chosen next," Chino said. "But first we need calm, or I get anxious and start killing more."

The people settled down; sniffles and quiet prayers whispered around the room.

"Good," Chino said and slung his gun over his shoulder. "We could all use a little God right now." He paused, allowing that statement to sink in. "Two people."

Ernesto walked around the reception hall and settled next to two old men. "You and you," he said with a poke of his weapon.

"Stand," Chino said.

The two men stood and tried to look brave in front of the faces of the evil before them.

"Show this to them," Ernesto said and slipped a cell phone into the back pocket of one of the men. "You guys are tasked to take that body out to them so they know we're not kidding."

"And you'll be free to go after that."

The two men picked up Sean's corpse, one grabbing him by the ankles and the other by the arms. His blood spilled from his body and left a long, thick trail that went out the door.

"El Rey de Imperio no tolerará tu asesinato de un inocente. Ese hombre es de su familia, Pecador."

"Who said that?" Chino said. He walked through the people, stepping over them like he was carefully navigating a landmine field.

The young man slowly stood with his hands raised. Ernesto, Chino, Sandra, and Manny aimed their weapons at him. The young man smiled, and Chino raised a hand, ordering his people to stand down.

"What did you say?" Chino said, moving close to him.

"The Empire Kings—"

"Wait," Chino said and circled away. "You a King?"

The man held his hands out, his fingers stacked in a gesture to show his affiliation.

"Well, lucky us," Chino said.

"No, not really," the Empire King said.

"How so?"

"You killed an innocent. Executed him in front of all these witnesses and cameras you have rolling. He was the cousin to—"

"I don't care," Chino said. "You and your gang . . . you've tried to move in on our territory. The Irish speaking Spanish, how flattering. Anyhow, that death is the price you pay for trespassing."

"You know as well as I do that there will be an answer." He paused and then raised his voice. "Vendetta."

Chino laughed and paced, quiet. "Then let us answer for two—it makes no difference to the Sinners." Chino nodded, and Sandra pulled the trigger to her automatic weapon.

Bap, bap, bap!

The bullets tore into the Empire King's body. He fell, and as he hit the ground, a white flash lit up the room and a concussive sound disoriented everyone.

Ringing in their ears drowned out the shouts of the police units that breached the reception hall's main room.

The police, dressed in tactical gear, entered the reception hall through the front, rear, and side entrances. The coordination of their plan had been carried out so well, the last shot fired had been from Sandra's gun when she shot her rival.

As the police locked down the scene, securing the Sinners and tending to the civilians, EMS workers along with fire rescue were able to evaluate the condition of the hostages.

Though no one other than the two dead men had sustained any injuries, torment from the Southside Sinners would be long lasting for the wedding guests. The remaining Empire Kings would especially never forget the Sinners' role in the events. And what happened this day would undoubtedly turn into an all-out war between the two factions.

CHAPTER 38

𝖜𝖔𝖒𝖆𝖓 𝖘𝖈𝖔𝖗𝖓𝖊𝖉

VICKI ENTERED THE precinct and quickly pulled out the weapon she'd concealed in her pocket. Shouts from the back could easily be identified as Urban's.

As a mother she innately knew the sound of her child when he was in distress. They had to be hurting him. He was frantic and at their mercy, most likely being treated like an animal.

She raced to the back and turned left, picking up speed when Urban's shouts grew louder. She was getting close to her baby. She missed him terribly.

"Get him out of here!" she heard an angry man's voice say. It had such a bite to it that it heated her blood.

Pressing onward, she finally reached the room where her son was shackled to the table. She aimed her weapon at the officers.

"Get the hell away from my son!" Vicki said.

Her eyes swept through the room quickly. Beto was at her feet, presumably dead from the amount of blood that surrounded his still body. That bitch officer was draped across a man's lap and was gasping for air. The pool of blood that surrounded her was even larger and darker than Beto's.

Then there were the three officers who surrounded her son. His face was bright red and streaked with tears. His hands were bound together and tethered to the table where he sat, chained like a dog.

"Get away from my boy I said!"

The officers raised their hands and took a slow step away.

"It's going to be OK now, Urban. Mommy has come to get you and take you away from these bad people."

"They shot Dad!"

"I see what they did. Don't look, baby," she said. She was talking to herself as much as her son. She looked at the female officer and waved the gun menacingly. "Get those damn cuffs off of him. Now!"

"You need to calm down," an officer said.

"Don't tell me what to do!" she shouted again. Her body shook, and the anger twisted her expression into something deadly.

"You better," Vicki said, her aim perfect, "better shut your mouth!"

Her finger hugged the trigger. Her heart pounded. She looked down and saw that Beto's blood had reached her feet.

"You people did this! One of you has to pay!"

Then, Vicki abruptly crumbled to the ground.

As Frerk slammed into Vicki, the gun discharged, firing wide.

Frerk wrestled her arms behind her back easily enough and cuffed her.

"Get off of my mother!"

Frerk stood and saw Creighton remove his red painted hands from his chest, his eyes hollow and in shock. He fell forward, draped over Emily.

Frerk and the three other officers hurried to Creighton's side only to see him gasp his last breath.

"Ha, ha!" Urban shouted. "That's what you get!"

CHAPTER 39

6 MONTHS LATER

"Push," Dr. Kellie Petticrew said.

Sweat beaded Hannah's forehead. Exhaustion from the long struggle pressed down on top of her. She was a prize fighter throwing the last haymakers to finish this off.

Her legs wide, a sheet covering her lower half, she listened as the doctor, between her legs, clad in full scrubs and a mask, spoke words of encouragement.

"C'mon, Hannah. One more push and the baby is out."

Hannah breathed in and out rapidly, hunkered down, and pushed. The baby slid out of the birth canal and into the doctor's hands. A nurse took the baby to the warming station, and the doctor looked at Hannah and nodded.

"Last push, and then you can rest."

"You said that the last time."

"You have one more, and then you can rest."

Hannah breathed heavily, held, pushed, and made this last effort mean everything.

"I see his head," Dr. Petticrew said. "He's coming!"

Those words encouraged Hannah to bring the next generation into this world. She growled, eager to hear the sounds of life.

"He's out," the doctor said, and another nurse came and took the baby and brought him to the warming station.

"Congratulations, Ms. Bebout, you have a healthy twin boy and girl."

Hannah rested and smiled. Tears streamed down her face.

Joy.

Tragedy.

Blessings.

Curses.

Repeat.

"Jennifer Stefanie Emily Bebout," Hannah said. "Rainer Glenn Bebout. That's their names."

"They're beautiful names," Dr. Petticrew said.

Hannah clung to the joy for a moment. "Please tell Eddie . . . my uncle, the godfather of these children, that they have come."

"We will do that. Now you concentrate on resting. Your work is yet to come, and you'll need your energy."

Hannah smiled. "I know." She fell into silence. "I wish my sister and parents were here to see this," she whispered and rested her head back, spent.

"THANK YOU FOR the flowers," Hannah said. Both joy and sadness clashed as she looked at the lush bouquet.

Paige rubbed her back. "I'm so sorry you have to live through this again."

Paige sat next to Hannah in the hospital bed. The room was private, and a uniformed officer was stationed outside the door.

"Thank you."

"And I'm glad you reached out to me. Everyone was so worried about you." Paige grabbed Hannah's hand. "No one knew where you were . . . if you were alive. When you didn't show for your sister's funeral, everyone thought the worst."

"I was told to stay away," Hannah said, her focus in her lap. "The Sinners." She licked her lips. "No one is sure if they're still active or not. They thought it best that I stay away. They wanted to make sure the twins were safe."

Paige squeezed Hannah's hand. "I'm glad to know you're OK."

"What they did to Jamie—"

"Don't," Paige said, and her eyes welled with tears.

"I'm sorry." Hannah sighed. "I'm sorry to anyone that got dragged into this. I wish you could tell her that."

"No one is to know where you are. People are beginning to heal once again from everything that happened. You are missed, but it is better this way."

"I know." Hannah looked at Paige. "I'm going to give these kids the best life possible."

"I know you will." Paige wiped her eyes and stood. "I'm going to get another look at them before I go."

Paige started toward the room's exit.

"Paige?"

She stopped and looked at Hannah.

"Thank you for being such a good friend over the years. I'm going to miss everyone. But I know this is for the best."

Paige nodded, turned away, and tears streamed down her face. She navigated the hallway, finding the nursery. She looked through the glass at the twins. They were so helpless and unknowing.

"I'm sorry," Paige said and raised her cell phone. She snapped a picture of the infants and prepared a text.

The children were born. They're staying at some guy's house named Eddie DePina in a town called Ardville. I've done what you've asked, now please leave my family alone.

She tapped the send button and exited the hos¬pital with a heavy heart, knowing full-well she'd put her own interests ahead of innocent children. She shook the thought away. Like the last time, she didn't have a choice.

CHAPTER 40

reemergence

URBAN SAT ON the corner of his bed in a room that didn't feel like it belonged to him. It felt like forever had gone by since they pulled him out of that holding room where that woman killed his father and his mother was taken from him.

Sleep was no friend of his, especially last night. When he tried to close his eyes all he could see was his father's face being blown to bits. The blood spray and the loud bang; the smell of gun smoke that was impossible to get out of his nose.

Today was a big day, and he was nervous for it. He looked out the window, and the day's bright sun gave him hope—something he hadn't had in a long time.

He went to his duffel bag on the floor, unzipped a side pocket, and took out the only picture he had of his mother. He had been hugging her, and she was smiling brightly, holding a beer in one hand and a cigarette in the other. He retreated to the bed.

He stared at the picture, and as he did so, a sudden rage filled his veins. He would be out of the system well before they ever released his mother from prison. He would go and visit her the very first day he got out, and she would be proud of him. Proud that he didn't just sit around and wallow in his misery.

The death of that officer wasn't her fault. It was the officer who had jumped her from behind. It was his actions that made the gun go off, killing the captain. But they had pinned it on his mom, and she had been convicted of murder. She wasn't eligible for parole until he reached the age of thirty-two. He'd lost everything because of the police.

All because of the woman who took him out of the house and stole him away from his parents. There was no doubt in his mind it was a premeditated event.

He studied the picture a little while longer and then turned it over. He took a pen, and with a neat hand he drew the 'SS,' and added the devil's tail to each one of the letters.

Just then, his phone vibrated, and he read the message. Yes, his mother would be proud of him indeed. He had become quite resourceful. Paige, the Empire Kings, and Hannah with the twins would come to know who he was and the rage in his heart for what they did to him. He would show them he was truly his father's son.

* * *

Next: The Cultures Collide series continues with the clash of the third generation and a new player, the Empire Kings!

about the author

KEITH ROMMEL is a self taught award-winning author and screen-writer. Writing in an array of different genres, Keith Rommel's work has been called "Horror for the curious mind" and "Thinking man's fiction." He lives in Florida with a ghost that keeps him company late into the night.